It's not fair!

"Did you see her take the money?" Daddy asked.

"I didn't see her, but no money's ever been stolen in our room—until Elsie came."

"All circumstantial evidence," Daddy announced importantly.

"What's that?" I asked.

"Just hearsay. You don't have solid proof. You just have Elsie under suspicion. You can't arrest her."

"It sounds like Elsie has enough troubles already." Mother started clearing the table as if the subject were closed.

"Mrs. Hanson said it isn't good for the thief not to be caught."

"Being accused wouldn't be good for Elsie if she wasn't the thief," Mother replied.

I didn't feel like doing my homework that night. I sat on my bed with my arithmetic book open to the page of fractions. I hate changing fractions to common denominators. I always get the numbers mixed up and backwards. I felt like sneaking downstairs to get the calculator. I wished I could call Diane. Most girls get to talk on the phone. My dad won't let me touch ours. It's not fair.

nothing's fair in fifth grade

Barthe DeClements

PUFFIN BOOKS

This book is dedicated to
my beloved son Christopher.

PUFFIN BOOKS

Published by the Penguin Group

Penguin Young Readers Group, 345 Hudson Street, New York, New York 10014, U.S.A.

Penguin Group (Canada), 90 Eglinton Avenue East, Suite 700, Toronto, Ontario, Canada M4P 2Y3
(a division of Pearson Penguin Canada Inc.)

Penguin Books Ltd, 80 Strand, London WC2R 0RL, England

Penguin Ireland, 25 St Stephen's Green, Dublin 2, Ireland (a division of Penguin Books Ltd)

Penguin Group (Australia), 250 Camberwell Road, Camberwell, Victoria 3124, Australia
(a division of Pearson Australia Group Pty Ltd)

Penguin Books India Pvt Ltd, 11 Community Centre, Panchsheel Park, New Delhi - 110 017, India

Penguin Group (NZ), 67 Apollo Drive, Rosedale, North Shore 0632, New Zealand
(a division of Pearson New Zealand Ltd)

Penguin Books (South Africa) (Pty) Ltd, 24 Sturdee Avenue,
Rosebank, Johannesburg 2196, South Africa

Registered Offices: Penguin Books Ltd, 80 Strand, London WC2R 0RL, England

First published in the United States of America by The Viking Press,
a member of Penguin Putnam, Inc., 1981

First published by Puffin Books, a division of Penguin Young Readers Group, 1990

This edition published by Puffin Books, a division of Penguin Young Readers Group, 2009

13 15 17 19 20 18 16 14

THE LIBRARY OF CONGRESS HAS CATALOGED THE VIKING EDITION AS FOLLOWS:

DeClements, Barthe.   Nothing's fair in fifth grade / by Barthe DeClements.   p.   cm.

Summary: Initially repelled by an overweight new student who has
serious home problems, the fifth grade class finally learns to accept her.

ISBN 978-0-670-51741-1 (hc)

[1. Weight control—Fiction. 2. Schools—Fiction.] I. Title.

[PZ7.D3584 No 1990] [Fic]—dc20 89-48757

Puffin Books ISBN 978-0-14-241349-4

Printed in the United States of America

Set in Times Roman

Contents

Contents

nothing's fair in fifth grade

The Fat Blond Girl

Mrs. Hanson, our fifth grade teacher, was sitting at her desk grading papers. We were all sitting at our desks. We were supposed to be writing paragraphs with one main sentence and three supporting sentences. I wrote down that my new kitten was soft, gray, and ten weeks old. Whatever else I wrote had to be about soft, gray, and ten weeks old. The fact that I couldn't teach it to go outside didn't match. The fact that if it went one more time on my mother's bed, I wouldn't have a kitten any more didn't match, either. I crumpled up my paper. I decided to write my main sentence about bratty little brothers. I could think of lots of supporting sentences for that.

I had just started my new paragraph when the classroom door opened and a woman and a fat blond girl walked in. Sharon sits behind me and I heard her say, "Ugh." Diane sits beside me and she whispered, "I hope she isn't going to be in this room."

The woman pushed the girl forward. "This is Elsie Edwards," she said.

"How are you, Elsie?" Mrs. Hanson asked.

"Fine," Elsie answered, looking at the floor.

Elsie's mother leaned over her and tried to talk quietly to Mrs. Hanson. We were all staring silently, though, and heard every word. Mrs. Edwards told Mrs. Hanson that Elsie was on a special diet. She was not to eat anything except what was in her lunch box. I thought to myself that it would take some special diet to melt off all that blubber.

When Elsie's mother left, Mrs. Hanson walked the fat girl to the front of the room. Elsie's hips were so wide her skirt brushed the desks on each side of the aisle. As she walked by Jack's desk, he shrank back from her in horror. A few kids giggled.

"Class," Mrs. Hanson said, "this is Elsie, our new student."

"You've got to be kidding," Roy muttered.

"She's gross," Diane said softly.

Elsie was gross. Her eyes were squished above cheek bubbles of fat. Her chins rippled down her neck. She really didn't have a waist except where her stomach bulged out below her chest. Her legs looked like two bed pillows with the ends stuffed in shoes. I knew everyone hated having Elsie in our room.

Diane sits on one side of me, but on the other side was the only empty desk in the room. My luck. Mrs. Hanson got some textbooks and brought Elsie to the empty desk. She said to me, "Jenifer, will you please show Elsie around the school at recess?"

I tried to agree politely, but I didn't like having my recess ruined. I always play with Diane and Sharon, so when Mrs. Hanson left, I whispered to Diane that she could help show Elsie around, too. Diane whispered back to forget it. So I was stuck with Elsie.

I showed Elsie where the bathroom was; I showed her the office, the gym, and the library. After our trip around the school, I asked her if she wanted to play a tetherball game. She said she'd rather watch, so I left her and went to find Diane and Sharon. Elsie leaned against the school building until the recess bell rang.

In P.E., Elsie told Mrs. Hanson she'd rather watch than play. Mrs. Hanson thought a minute and then said she supposed it would be all right for Elsie's first day. Elsie sat on the stage steps and watched us bombard each other in a soak 'em game.

Elsie didn't just watch at lunchtime, though. She hunched over her desk and gobbled up her carrot, thermos of soup, and pear in three minutes. When she was finished, she leaned across and asked me if I wanted my cornbread. Cornbread is the one thing the school cooks don't ruin. But I pulled my bread apart and gave Elsie a fourth of it.

"Thanks," Elsie mumbled as she stuffed it in her mouth. While she was chewing, she looked at Sharon's lunch tray. Sharon was talking to Diane, who was holding her short black hair away from her face while she drank her milk from a straw. Elsie reached out and poked Sharon in the side.

"Are you going to eat your dessert?" she asked.

"Yes, I am," Sharon answered and turned back to Diane.

Elsie put her thermos in her lunch box and wadded up her paper napkin. She got up to throw her napkin in the wastebasket. On the way back she stopped at Marianne's desk. Marianne's cornbread was on her tray. Marianne was watching Jack cut up milk straws for spit wad shooters.

"Say, are you going to eat your cornbread?" Elsie asked. Marianne continued to watch Jack.

Elsie didn't know Marianne's name so she poked her in the arm. "Are you going to eat your cornbread?"

Marianne, surprised, looked up at Elsie. She shoved

the tray forward. "No, take it," she said.

Elsie stuffed Marianne's cornbread in her mouth and began to weave her way back to her seat. It was a close squeeze between Richard's desk and Jack's desk. Richard's books slid to the floor.

"Hey, watch it!" Richard yelled.

Mrs. Hanson looked up. As Elsie stopped to pick up the books, her skirt billowed behind her. Jack raised his hand to smack the huge target.

"Jack!" Mrs. Hanson said sharply. Jack put his hand down slowly. Mrs. Hanson asked Elsie what she was eating.

Elsie swallowed. "Lunch."

"Whose lunch?" Mrs. Hanson wanted to know.

"It's just some cornbread," Elsie said. Her cheeks had turned red, and the color dripped down her chins. Everyone was watching.

"Elsie, your mother said you were on a strict diet. In this room you eat only what your mother puts in your lunch box. Do you understand?" Mrs. Hanson looked directly into Elsie's eyes.

"But I get so hungry," Elsie whimpered. She sneaked a look around the room. I didn't feel sorry for her. I was glad she was getting it. She was so gross.

Elsie added, "I only get some broth, a carrot, and a pear in my lunch."

"I'm sorry if you get hungry, Elsie, but this is something you'll have to take up with your mother and your doctor." Mrs. Hanson turned away from Elsie and told us to clean up the room.

After lunch it was raining, so we couldn't go out on the playfield. Elsie stood against the school building again while the rest of us gathered under the covered area talking about her. Sharon said she should be in a circus, and Diane said she should be a garbage collector. I glanced over at Elsie while everyone giggled at the jokes. Elsie stood there silently with the wind flapping her tentlike coat around her. I thought her mouth turned down sadly.

When I got home from school, the whole kitchen smelled of chocolate chip cookies. I draped my wet jacket over a chair, opened cupboard doors until I found the stack, and helped myself to four.

Mother looked up from peeling potatoes. "Jenifer!"

I put one back and sat down at the kitchen table to eat the rest. My little brother, Kenny, hovered around me, whispering, "Me, too, Jenny," so I figured Mother must have told him no more. When the whispering didn't work, he climbed up the rungs of my chair and patted my long hair. I broke off a piece of cookie and gave it to him. He gave me his pumpkin-teeth grin in return.

While I watched Mother cut up the potatoes, I told her about Elsie.

"I wonder why she eats so much," Mother said.

I thought that was a strange question. Didn't Elsie eat because she was hungry?

A Sports Car Holds Only Two

At noon the next day Elsie had her lunch box cleaned before I even got my hot lunch tray into the classroom. She sat with her hands folded, staring first at Sharon and then at me. Halfway through the lunch period Mr. Douglas, the principal, walked in. He's a great big, joking man. At least he is if you aren't a troublemaker. He walked around the room asking kids how they liked their lunches. When he came to Elsie, he said, "And where's your lunch, young lady?"

"I ate it." She never really looked at grown-ups, but kept her face pointing down.

"I hope it was good." He patted her on the shoulder and went on up the aisle.

While I licked a smear of frosting from my fingers, I watched Elsie watching the teacher. When Mrs. Hanson bent her head to stir her tea, Elsie leaned back toward Sharon. "Are you going to eat your cake?"

"Yes, I am," Sharon answered, pulling her tray closer to her chest.

Elsie turned to Marianne. "Are you going to eat your cake?"

Marianne is the littlest girl in the room. She isn't very smart, but she's nice to everyone. "You can have half," Marianne said.

Elsie took the piece of cake and jammed it in her mouth. Mrs. Hanson was at Elsie's desk in a flash.

"Elsie, what are you doing?"

Elsie was so surprised her mouth flopped open with the hunk of chocolate cake hanging on her lower teeth.

"Elsie, spit that out into the wastebasket, and don't let me catch you disobeying me again." Mrs. Hanson's voice was so sharp I shivered.

Elsie spit the cake into the wastebasket while we all craned our necks to watch her. When she was back at her desk, she took out her reading book, opened it to the middle, and stared at the pages. Mrs. Hanson and the principal stood at the front of the room talking quietly. Then Mr. Douglas went over to Elsie and put his hand on her shoulder again.

"Young lady," he said, "you'd better straighten up and start behaving in this school. We won't put up with any of your antics *here*."

I wasn't certain what he meant by antics, but I wondered what Elsie had done in her other school.

After that day the boys started calling Elsie "Scrounge." And she was the classroom reject.

My mother says I should be nice to everyone. Either school was different when she was young or she just doesn't remember. I'm not a mean girl, but I do have best friends. There are girls like Marianne who will play with anyone and everyone still likes them. There's nothing to hate about Marianne. She's little and friendly and she will lend you anything. My mother says Marianne has character. I told my mother Marianne works all day and only gets C's. Mother said grades aren't everything. She says things like that, but when I bring home my report card, I better have only A's and B's.

So Marianne talked to Elsie, but nobody else went near her. Elsie kept standing by the school wall at recess. She hardly moved unless she saw some kid who had sneaked candy out on the playground. Then she walked right up and asked for a piece. She couldn't scrounge at lunchtime, because Mrs. Hanson watched her like a hawk. Mrs. Hanson didn't pick on kids for no reason, but she could hang right on you if you were doing something bad. The only one she had trouble catching was Jack. Most of the time he was just too sneaky for her.

One day when Elsie had been in our room a few weeks, Mrs. Hanson said we would work in groups for globe study. There were seven world globes, so that meant four students would share each globe. Mrs. Hanson called on Marianne to choose the first group. Marianne chose me and Diane. Next she should have chosen Sharon because we're friends, but she didn't. She chose Elsie. I opened my mouth to object, but closed it fast when I saw Mrs. Hanson eyeing me.

Our group sat on the floor by the teacher's desk. The ditto work sheets listed the latitude and longitude of six cities. We were supposed to find the cities on the globe and write down their names. Diane was the smartest in social studies, so she found most of the cities and we finished before any of the other groups.

I told Diane what happened on *Mork and Mindy* the night before because her TV was broken. To be polite, Marianne asked Elsie what movies she'd seen lately. Elsie said her little sister and her mother had seen a show over the weekend, but she didn't go.

"How come you didn't go?" Diane asked.

"Mama has a sports car and it holds only two," Elsie said.

"Then you get to go next time," Marianne said.

"I don't think so." Elsie shook her head slowly.

"Why not?" Diane asked.

"Well, Mama says I'm big enough to stay home alone and my little sister isn't," Elsie explained.

"That's dumb," Diane said. "Why doesn't she get a baby-sitter for your little sister?"

"She does sometimes, but not to take me."

"Why not?" Diane persisted.

"I don't think she wants anyone to know I belong to her. I'm too fat, I guess."

I watched Elsie separate a yellow curl from the rest of her hair, twirl it around a thick finger, and yank on it. I guess Marianne saw this, too, because she suddenly asked me how my kitten was doing. I told her she had a sleeping box on the back porch. She had to stay outside all the time except when I was playing with her.

"I bet Mama would like to do that with me," Elsie said.

I told my mother about Elsie and her mother. Mother said, "Poor little thing."

I said, "Mother, she's no *little* thing."

The Finger Points

Whenever I brought lunch money to school, I put it in my desk or sometimes I left it *on* my desk, even though I knew I wasn't supposed to. Nobody had ever taken anything in our room. And if I kept my money in my pocket, I could lose it.

If you lose your money, the school won't give you a free lunch. The teachers won't lend you money, either. What you have to do is go to the office and get a frozen peanut butter sandwich from the secretary. She keeps a whole bunch of them in the refrigerator in the faculty room. It's a pain because they never completely thaw in time for lunch. Some kids just go hungry instead of trying to eat the secretary's sandwiches. I guess the school figures this cuts down on kids' forgetting their lunch money.

Halfway through that fifth grade year there was no money out on anyone's desk. Quarters were disappearing every day. Marianne was the first to lose money. I thought it was just an accident. I guess Mrs. Hanson did, too. She told Marianne to look through her desk. Marianne did, but she ended up with a peanut butter sandwich. Some kids gave her their cookies and Jack gave her his milk. He told her he didn't like milk, but I know he always drank it before.

The next day Roy's money was gone. He missed it right after recess. He took out all the junk from his desk and spread it all over the floor. It took him till lunchtime to sift through the mess, but he ended up with a peanut butter sandwich, too.

The third day Diane's money was missing. Now, Diane isn't messy and she isn't forgetful and she isn't the type to be quiet about getting a peanut butter sandwich in place of a hot lunch.

"I put my money right here in my desk," Diane said clearly. "It was here before recess and it isn't here now. Somebody stole it!"

"Diane, you don't know that," Mrs. Hanson said.

Diane looked up at her. "Where are my quarters, then?"

I thought Mrs. Hanson would really give it to her for being rude. Instead she just told her to go through her desk once more. Diane pursed her lips, gave a big impatient sigh, and kneeled down by her desk. Mrs. Hanson kneeled down, too—not to look in Diane's desk, but to look in the one in front of it—Richard's. Maybe Richard took the money.

As she poked around in his desk, Richard jumped out of his seat. "Hey, I ain't a thief."

"Am not!" Mrs. Hanson corrected him. "And I didn't say you were. Empty your pants pockets."

Richard yanked out the lining of his empty pants pockets.

Mrs. Hanson moved back to search my desk. I felt my face burn as I remembered I sat behind Roy, who had lost his money, and beside Diane, who had lost her money. I didn't sit by Marianne, though. I hoped none of the kids thought I stole the money.

Mrs. Hanson held out her hand. "Let me see your purse."

I gave her my purse. She looked through it carefully. The only money that was in it was the fifty cents for my lunch. I was lucky I didn't have my birthday money in it.

Diane stood up and crossed her arms. Her black eyes glittered. "There is no money anywhere in my desk."

Mrs. Hanson gave me back my purse. "Do you have a purse, Diane?" she asked.

"No, I don't," Diane said.

"Go look in your coat pockets."

Diane stamped over to the girls' coat closet, took down her coat, and pulled out the pockets. Except for a wad of Kleenex, they were empty.

"Diane," Mrs. Hanson said, "are you certain you brought your lunch money to school?"

"Yes, I am," Diane answered.

Mrs. Hanson looked around at the whole class. "If Diane brought her money into this classroom, it must still be here. I don't think we'll have lunch until we find Diane's money."

I stuffed my books back in my desk. This was going to be a disaster. I don't know why teachers do this. Who would ever tell after all that fuss?

When we heard the lunch cart in the hall, Mrs. Hanson sat down at her desk. "I guess we'll just be hungry until the money turns up," she said.

It didn't work. We sat there in silence until one of the cooks stuck her head in the room and said we'd have to line up for lunch right away or the lunch cart would leave for the sixth grade unit. Mrs. Hanson lined us up. I wondered if she'd keep us after school. She didn't.

I was still mad at Mrs. Hanson when I walked home with Diane and Sharon. I thought it was mean of her to make me look like a thief. Sharon said she didn't think it was mean, because I did sit by Roy and Diane and, besides, Mrs. Hanson had looked in Richard's desk, too. I got upset all over again and started hollering that where we sat didn't make any difference. Diane said to cool it. What really mattered was who was taking the money. Diane thought it might be Jack. I didn't think so because Jack had given Marianne his milk.

"Maybe he figured he owed it to her," Sharon suggested.

"I think it's Elsie," I said.

"No," Diane said, "her mother looks like they're loaded with money."

"That doesn't mean she gives Elsie any," I argued. "She said her mother hates her."

"She didn't say her mother hates her," Diane corrected me.

"Well, her mother's ashamed of her. Anyway, if her mother gave her a dollar, she'd probably buy a cake."

"True," said Diane.

When I got home, I followed my mother around the kitchen while she made dinner. I was all wound up and wanted her to listen to the whole story. I told her Mrs. Hanson practically accused Richard and me of stealing.

My mother asked me, "Did you take the money?"

Anger just swooshed over me. "What are you talking about!" I screamed at her. "Do you think I steal?"

I ran up to my room and slammed the door.

She came up later to tell me dinner was ready. I told her I didn't want any. My mother said quietly that she had simply asked me a question about taking the money. She hadn't accused me of anything. I didn't look at her. She went away. I turned on my radio. I was starving.

I was on my bed staring at the ceiling when Kenny pushed open my door.

"Jenny, why don't you want to eat?" he asked.

"Get out of here!" I yelled. I dashed over to the door and shoved him out. Hard.

To Catch a Thief

I expected the next day to be miserable, too. It wasn't. It was a neat day. Mrs. Hanson chose Diane and me to put up the fifth grade art in the gym for Open House that night.

At morning recess all the kids were still talking about the class thief. I felt relieved because we girls were in a big circle by the tetherball, and I knew no one would be talking about it with me if they suspected me. Most everyone thought it was Elsie. Money had never disappeared before Elsie came. I turned around to see where she was.

"Hey," I burst out. "Elsie isn't standing by the wall!"

"I bet she's in the room stealing money," Diane said. "Let's get her."

Our group marched together to the front of the fifth grade unit. Just as we got to the door, Elsie came out.

"Elsie, where have you been?" Diane demanded.

"I was in the bathroom," Elsie said. "What's it to you?"

Diane moved up close to her. "You aren't supposed to go in during recess unless you get a pass from the playground teacher."

"That's stupid. What is recess for?" Elsie looked Diane straight in the eye and then turned and waddled off.

She had a point. It always seemed dumb to me that you couldn't go to the bathroom at recess. Why didn't the teachers just lock the classroom doors? When I said this, though, Sharon pointed out that the school would have to put a teacher aide in every unit or the kids would have water all over the place. That's true. Even third graders know how to flood the toilets.

After lunch recess we didn't have our regular reading. On the day of Open House all the kids have to clean out their desks and scrub off all the words. There's a lot of water and confusion and noise. Boys like Jack manage to squirt some water around, and the teacher gets crabby and gives everyone two pages of long division to get the room calmed down.

But Diane and I didn't have to be part of all that. As soon as we got back to the classroom, we took the pile of pictures Mrs. Hanson had been collecting from the class and went to the gym. On the way we talked about the thief. Everyone had lunch or lunch money that day, so I thought Elsie wasn't the thief. Diane said maybe all the kids took their money out to recess and there wasn't any money left in the room for Elsie to steal. That was possible.

Two sixth grade boys were in the gym stapling pictures to the wall. It was Chris Johnson and Mark Howard. They're the cutest boys in the sixth grade, and Diane and I got all nervous. Diane didn't show it, though. She just asked in a bossy voice where we were supposed to put our pictures since the boys were taking up the whole wall. Chris Johnson said there were four walls.

We chose the wall under the basketball hoop. When the boys finished with their pictures, they got the basketball out and started tossing baskets. The ball accidentally bounced off my shoulder. I turned around.

"Oops, sorry," Mark said and grinned.

I knew I was going to smile back, so I quickly faced the wall.

"Hey," Chris asked, "who's that blimp in your room?"

Diane said it was Elsie, and we started talking to the boys about her. They used their stapler to help us finish the pictures. They said since they helped us get done so fast we should play a game of keep-away with them. We did. We were having so much fun I was shocked when I heard the last bell ring.

"We'd better split," Diane said.

We hurried and picked up our staplers and headed for our unit. I was worried because some of the classes were already coming out of their rooms. When we got to our room, the kids weren't even lined up to go home. The room was spotless. Mrs. Hanson was collecting math papers. Just as I thought. Mrs. Hanson told Diane and me to get our folders and place them on our desks. I made a pretty semicircle with mine. I was glad I had only good papers for my parents to see.

When I got home from school, my kitten was jumping around the kitchen, trying to swat a moth.

"How come she's not outside?" I asked my mother.

She looked up from the meat loaf she was mixing and smiled. "She finally got the idea."

"No kidding?" I sat down on the floor and took the gray fluffy thing in my lap. "What does she do?"

"She goes to the door and meows."

"Fantastic! I'm going to call her D.D."

"Why D.D.?" Mother wanted to know.

"Because kids who get D's are slow to catch on. Can I take D.D. up to my room?"

"Sure. Just put her out fast if she meows at your door. Listen, take a bath, will you, and put on your birthday blouse. Remember, we're all going to Open House right after dinner."

I stopped cold at the kitchen door. "Kenny, too?"

Mother put up her meat-loafy hands. "Don't worry. He's still napping. I put him down late, so he'll be good. He's all excited about going to school and getting to sit at your desk."

"Sit at my desk? Great! If he has to go, he better meow at the door."

"Now, Jenny, he hasn't had an accident in months."

"You mean weeks."

It was fun to joke with my mother again. We usually are friends. But I still didn't think she should have asked me if I had stolen the money. She should have known I wouldn't.

I thought about that as I poured some of her lemon bath oil into the bath water. I rolled up a wad of toilet paper for D.D. to bat around while I was in the tub. I climbed in and slunk way down until the bubbles touched my chin.

It was sort of a miracle that D.D. suddenly got trained. I bet my mother did it while I was at school to make up for not trusting me. Maybe that's also why Mrs. Hanson chose Diane and me to take the art work to the gym.

There was a funny noise. Meow! I jumped out of the

tub, threw a towel over me, grabbed D.D., and dashed for the stairs.

Mother laughed as I flew through the kitchen to the back door. I put D.D. on the porch and watched. D.D. jumped down the steps, tail straight up, and headed for Mother's flower beds.

Kenny was on his best behavior when our family arrived at school. Mother and Dad found Sharon's parents, and we all went to our classroom together. My folks and Sharon's are friends. Sometimes our families go camping together. I try to have fun with Sharon when Diane isn't along. It isn't easy. Sharon is interested in two things—what her mother says and how many presents she can pile up. You'd think she was an only child instead of Diane.

Sharon pranced right up to Diane and her mother so they could admire her new pink dress. She had a matching pink barrette in her hair. I have to admit her curly hair is pretty. It's blond, like Elsie's. Only Elsie's fat face makes hers look stuck on like a wig. I didn't see Elsie or her mother at Open House.

While my parents were looking through my folders and my brother was sitting at my desk, Mrs. Hanson came over. I was surprised at how nice she looked. Her gray hair was waved, and she had red earrings on. She told Dad I was a good student. Mother was busy reading one of my English stories. I am good in English. I am *exceptionally* good in English, my mother says. I am not so good in math. Fortunately for me, all the papers in my arithmetic folder were C or better.

On the way home Kenny said I had a "smiley teacher."

"That was just for Open House," I told him.

My mother said she wouldn't want to be that age and try to hold down a bunch of ten- and eleven-year-olds. My father said he wouldn't want to do it at any age. He asked me about the kid with the red hair.

"That's Jack," I told him. "He hates his red hair."

"I bet he's a handful," Daddy said.

The next day it happened again. Lester's lunch money disappeared. I was glad he sat way in the back corner of the room, so no one would think I took his two quarters.

Mrs. Hanson asked him where he had put his lunch money.

"Right in plain sight on my desk," Lester said.

She closed her eyes a minute. "That wasn't very intelligent of you," she said.

"Well, I had it where I could watch it," he explained.

"When did you last see the two quarters?" she asked.

"Right before recess."

"Did you leave them on your desk while you were out at recess?"

"Sure," he said.

She closed her eyes again.

I have to admit that wasn't very bright. My mother had given me an extra dollar in the morning to buy a quart of milk at the 7-Eleven on my way home from school. I had it pinned inside my jeans' pocket.

Mrs. Hanson told Lester he'd have to get a peanut butter sandwich from the office for his lunch. Lester slumped down in his seat.

After lunch recess Mrs. Hanson pulled her chair to the front of the room and sat down. She looked at us. We looked back at her.

"We have a problem in this room," she began slowly. "I don't think money disappearing four times can be called an accident. I don't like to say this to you, but I think someone in this room is taking the money."

She stopped. We didn't make a sound.

"Now generally, as you know, I don't like tattling. But this is different. This is serious. Helping to find out who is taking the money is not tattling. Whoever is doing it has a problem. It doesn't help that person to let him get away with it. Him *or* her." She stopped again.

For the first time that year I liked her. It seemed like she was on our side.

She went on. "If anyone knows something or has seen something that has to do with the money, please tell me you want to talk to me. We'll talk alone and I won't tell anyone about it."

That's all she said. The rest of the afternoon we read quietly in our reading books. Just before the last bell rang, the principal came in. He asked us for our attention.

"Mrs. Hanson has informed me that someone in this room is taking money. Now, every person makes mistakes. But it takes a strong person to come forward and say he made a mistake.

"I think I know who took the money." He looked all around the room. I watched to see if his eyes stopped on anyone, but they didn't. "If that student is a strong person, he or she will come to Mrs. Hanson or to me and admit to making a mistake. Now, I want you students to think about that."

We thought about it. After school we stood in groups outside the building and talked about it, but no one seemed to know anything. Finally I had to leave to go to the 7-Eleven to buy the milk for my mother.

There was a stack of new comic books in the store. I stopped at the magazine rack to look through them before I got the milk. I started reading parts of *Charlie Brown,* but somebody kept moving behind me at the candy rack, nudging me closer to the magazines. It interrupted my reading.

I turned around to see who was bothering me. I saw Elsie's fat back. No wonder there wasn't enough room. I stood there watching her. She was carefully picking out the longest red and black licorice whips. When she had five of them, she went to the cashier's counter.

I stuck *Charlie Brown* back on the shelves and whipped down the aisle to get the milk. I wanted to see the money Elsie used to pay for the candy. She was next in line when I got to the counter. Just as I thought. She plunked down two quarters!

When the clerk handed her the bag of candy, I said, "Hi, Elsie."

She looked up, stared straight at me with her eyes wide, then left the store without saying a word. I knew I had looked into the eyes of a thief.

I couldn't wait to get home and tell Mother. I wondered if I should call Mrs. Hanson or the principal. I wished I could stop at Diane's house to tell her what happened.

Mother took the milk out of my hands as soon as I got in the door. She looked cross. "What took you so long?"

"I saw Elsie in the 7-Eleven and she was buying candy . . ."

"And I suppose you waited around to get some." She looked at the milk. "Jenifer Sawyer! This is nonfat milk!"

"Oh, I'm sorry. I guess I didn't read the carton."

"Jenifer, you and Kenny are too skinny already. You don't need nonfat milk."

"I'll go back and exchange it," I said.

"No, it's too late now. Go get washed for dinner."

She sure was in a crabby mood. All my excitement drained away.

At dinner Daddy talked about inflation. He didn't know how we were ever going to afford a new car. Mother said she couldn't save anything; food was going up every day. Big news. I waited until dessert for an opening.

"Money's being stolen in our classroom," I said.

"We know," Mother replied.

I ignored her. "I think I found out who's taking it."

"How?" Daddy asked me.

"I saw Elsie at the 7-Eleven, buying candy. She's on a diet. She isn't supposed to be eating candy. She paid with two quarters, and that's exactly what was stolen from Lester today."

"How does that prove Elsie took the money?" Daddy asked.

"Because Elsie's mother never gives her money. She knows she'd spend it on food."

"I bet her grandma gave her money!" Kenny butted in.

"You stay out of this," I told him.

"Well, maybe her grandmother did," Mother said.

"No, you don't understand. We saw Elsie in the fifth grade unit during recess. And recess is when the money gets stolen."

"Did you see her take the money?" Daddy asked.

"I didn't see her, but no money's ever been stolen in our room—until Elsie came."

"All circumstantial evidence," Daddy announced importantly.

"What's that?" I asked.

"Just hearsay. You don't have solid proof. You just have Elsie under suspicion. You can't arrest her."

"I don't want to arrest her! Anyway, Mrs. Hanson said we were to tell her if we saw any little thing."

"It sounds like Elsie has enough troubles already." Mother started clearing the table as if the subject were closed.

"Mrs. Hanson said it isn't good for the thief not to be caught."

"Being accused wouldn't be good for Elsie if she wasn't the thief," Mother replied.

I didn't feel like doing my homework that night. I sat on my bed with my arithmetic book open to the page of fractions. I hate changing fractions to common denominators. I always get the numbers mixed up and backwards. I felt like sneaking downstairs to get the calculator. I wished I could call Diane. Most girls get to talk on the phone. My dad won't let me touch ours. It's not fair.

The Office Jail

The next morning Diane, Sharon, and I walked to school, figuring out what to do about Elsie. Diane thought I should go right smack to the principal's office. Sharon thought I should tell Mrs. Hanson I wanted a conference with her. I couldn't decide what to do. The closer I got to school, the more my breakfast lumped in my stomach.

"The terrible threesome!" a boy's voice called out behind us.

"Which one do you think's the cutest?" another boy asked.

"Oh, I don't know. Depends on if you like short hair, long hair, or curly hair."

We girls glanced at each other. We knew it was Chris Johnson and Mark Howard. In the girls' bathroom where we went to comb our hair, Sharon asked the mirror, "Which do *you* think is the cutest?"

"Mark is the fairest of them all," Diane announced.

"I think Chris is," I said.

"You would," Diane said, putting Chapstick on her lips. We weren't allowed to use lipstick. Chapstick made our lips shiny. Diane passed it around.

I was at my desk watching Elsie fit her body into her seat before I remembered that I hadn't talked to Mrs. Hanson or the principal about the licorice whips.

Mrs. Hanson started class by telling us to take out our arithmetic papers and pass them to the person behind us. I shrugged my shoulders when Sharon poked me in the back for my paper. After the papers were corrected, Mrs. Hanson asked for our scores. Sharon said, "Zero," when my name was called. Mrs. Hanson stopped with her pencil above her grade book and peered at me. I know I turned red. Elsie got her usual one hundred.

I was poky about getting my coat on at recess. I thought I'd wait around while the other kids went out and maybe get a chance to say something to Mrs. Hanson. But she herded us all quickly out the door, locked it with her key, and went off to the faculty room.

At lunch I sat chewing my hot dog bun and wondering if Elsie would get away free. If Mrs. Hanson locked the door every day that might be the end of the stealing. I looked over at Elsie and saw she was chewing on a licorice whip.

Mrs. Hanson saw her, too. She came up behind Elsie and took the whip out of her hand. "What is this?"

"It's mine," Elsie said.

"Where did you get it?"

"It was in my lunch box."

"In your lunch box? Are you sure?"

"Yes."

"Are you sure you didn't buy it?"

"No, I don't have any money." Elsie kept her eyes on the licorice whip dangling above her.

I raised my hand. Mrs. Hanson ignored me.

"I'll just keep this for now and give your mother a call," Mrs. Hanson said. "If she's changed your diet, I want to know about it."

I put my hand down. Elsie was going to get it for sure.

At lunch recess Diane decided she would do something about Elsie's taking her money. Otherwise, she said, she'd never get it back. She marched up to Elsie with Sharon and me trailing behind.

"So, Elsie," she said sarcastically, "that licorice whip came in your lunch box."

"What's it to you, Diane?"

"It's plenty to me, Elsie. I got cheated out of my lunch because of you. You owe me fifty cents!"

"You have lots of money," Elsie mumbled.

"Oh, you think so, huh?" Diane tossed her head back, flicking her bangs out of her eyes. "Well, my mother's a widow and she works for our money. We don't even have ten dollars to fix our TV. So you just give me my money, Elsie Edwards."

"How come you have so many dresses and pants if you're so poor?"

"Because my grandma's a good sewer, that's why. Now give me my money!"

Elsie looked up at the sky. "I don't have any money," she said.

"Come off it. Your mother isn't poor and you know it."

"That doesn't mean I have any money." Elsie kept looking up, and then I figured out why. She was trying to keep from crying.

The playground teacher came over and asked what we were doing.

"Just talking," Diane said.

"Let's get into a game." The playground teacher took Diane's hand.

Diane jerked loose. "Is there a school rule against talking at recess?"

"Listen, missy, sometimes you're too smart-mouthed for your own good."

The bell rang. Elsie moved toward the classroom. The playground teacher had to go back to the field to blow her whistle.

"Gee, Diane," Sharon said, "you could get yourself in trouble."

Diane shrugged. "Oh, she's just a teacher's aide."

The boys in our class came over and wanted to know what was going on.

"I was just trying to get my money back from that thief Elsie," Diane told them.

"Elsie's the thief?" Lester said. "That scrounge! We should beat her up."

"Go ahead and beat her up," Jack told Lester. "If she falls on you, you'll be smashed dead."

While we were doing oral reading, the principal came into the room. He walked down the middle aisle to Elsie's desk.

"You come with me, young lady," he said to Elsie. Then he turned to Mrs. Hanson and said, "This young lady won't be back for a while."

Mrs. Hanson nodded. "All right, Mr. Douglas, that will be fine."

Elsie didn't come back all afternoon.

After school we saw a fancy sports car in the visitors' parking lot.

"I bet she's in the office," Diane said.

So Sharon, Diane, and I trooped back to the building and peeked in the principal's window. The blinds were closed, but we could see through the slits. Sure enough. There sat the principal, Elsie's mother, and Elsie. Elsie didn't look too happy. Neither did Mrs. Edwards. She was pointed straight up in her chair like a missile ready for take off.

"Elsie got caught today," I crowed at my mother when I got home.

"What happened?" my mother asked.

"You know that candy I told you she bought at the 7-Eleven? She ate it in school, and Mrs. Hanson asked her where she got it. Elsie said it was in her lunch box. Mrs. Hanson said she'd call her mother. Then we saw Elsie and her mother with the principal in the principal's office after school."

"Well, that doesn't prove she took the money."

"Really, Mother," I said and scooped up D.D. to play with in my room.

After dinner I didn't feel like doing my arithmetic again. I tried doing some of the problems and got them all wrong. I forgot how to change my answers to mixed numbers. I wished I were one of the kids who could finish the assignment at school.

I went downstairs to ask Mother to help me. First she fiddled around putting Kenny to bed, and then she picked up all his toys from the floor.

"Why don't you make Kenny do that? He's not a baby any more." I was tired of waiting for her.

Daddy looked up from his paper. "I thought I heard you ask your mother to help you. If you're in a hurry, why don't you help her?"

I picked up Kenny's truck and lugged it to his play-box.

Mother sat down on the davenport and opened my book. "I'd better read the directions first. The school's always changing the math."

"It's just fractions," I told her crossly.

Daddy looked up again. Silently I waited for her to read through the three pages.

"Oh, it's the same as I remember. When you have an improper fraction in your answer, you divide the numerator by the denominator and add the whole number to the number you already have."

"Whaat?" I said.

"Look, I'll show you." She showed me three times. I sort of caught on.

"Here, we'll try a problem now." She wrote out $15\frac{3}{4} - 3\frac{6}{15}$.

I got it all mixed up, of course. I dropped the pencil on the floor.

"I'll never get it. It isn't fair. That thief Elsie always gets a hundred."

"I don't like to hear you call her that, Jenifer," Mother said. "She's just a girl who's got a lot of problems."

"You mean she's just a girl who's giving a lot of people problems."

"If you're going to argue, go up to your room," my father said. "We don't need that down here."

I took my book and went up to my room. I lay down on my bed. I felt awful. I was tired. I wished I hadn't eaten two pieces of fried chicken for dinner. I could taste them. I dragged my clothes off slowly, didn't brush my teeth or wash my face. I got into bed and pulled the covers over me.

I shivered. I thought of those TV commercials where the man's stomach balloons in and out and his face turns green. His pill wouldn't have helped me. I knew what I had. The flu. I wanted to tell Mother, but I felt too weak to get out of bed. I knew I was going to throw up pretty soon. I wished it would hurry up.

I made it to the bathroom, barely. I was on the bathroom floor with sweat running down my forehead when Mother came in.

"Oh, honey, you're sick." She got a washcloth and wiped my forehead with cold water. She helped me back to bed and brought a towel, a glass of water, and a pan to put beside me.

"Do you want anything else?"

I shook my head. I just wanted to die.

I stayed that way for four days. Mother would come in and coax me to drink water or juice. I'd drink it and throw up. The doctor came. He told Mother I was de-hydrated—that means dried out. He said if I couldn't keep fluids down in the next twenty-four hours he'd feel better if I was in the hospital.

After he left, I asked Mother what good it would do to be in a hospital. Mother said they would feed me intravenously—that meant with a needle stuck in my arm.

I took a sip of apple juice, lay on my back, and waited. It came up. I took another sip of apple juice, lay on my back, and waited. It came up. I took a tinier sip of apple juice, lay on my back, and waited and waited and waited. It stayed down.

It was two days before I felt strong enough to be propped up on pillows and read a book—and it wasn't the arithmetic book. On the third day Mother wobbled into my room in her nightgown to ask me if I thought I could manage alone. I took one look at her stringy hair and white face and told her I'd be fine. She wobbled back to bed.

Kenny brought me my breakfast. It was three pieces of toast piled with jam, a glass of milk, and a bowl of applesauce. It tasted good.

He tried to give Mother breakfast, but that didn't work. He brought her an empty pan instead. To enter-tain me, Kenny stacked his picture books on my bed and read me *Green Eggs and Ham* from memory. The phone rang in the afternoon. Kenny ran to answer it. It was Diane wanting to talk to me I took my first trip downstairs in a week.

Diane was chock-full of school news. We talked for an hour. I didn't hear a peep from upstairs. I guess Mother wasn't in any condition to object.

Diane gave me all the latest on Elsie. She said Elsie had to sit in the office during every morning recess and lunch recess. She wasn't ever allowed to be alone in the school building. Mrs. Hanson didn't have to lock the classroom door any more. Diane said she met a girl from Elsie's old school at a church skating party. The girl said Elsie had stolen at that school. Only there she mostly stole food. They even caught her in the school kitchen eating up the cinnamon rolls. Diane said the kids hated Elsie at her old school, too.

I wasn't the only one with the flu. A whole bunch of kids were absent. Diane said that Elsie was out, Marianne was out, and Jack was out. Diane wanted to know when I'd be back. I guessed in a couple of days.

It was more than that because the next day Kenny was sick. I took care of him till Mother could get up.

Fat Girls Can't Dance

School was the same when I got back. Mrs. Hanson was still strict. Jack was well again and throwing crayons. Elsie was back, too, fat as ever.

The school was having a yearly clean-up campaign. We drew "Don't Litter" posters in the morning. In the afternoon our class had to clean up the south playfield. Mrs. Hanson said Marianne, Elsie, Jack, and I were to go to the library instead of picking up litter. She said it was too chilly outside for us.

Jack sat in the back of the library. Marianne and I chose a front table. Elsie plopped herself in the middle chair, which meant Marianne and I had to move our chairs out to give her body room. Elsie read a library book. Marianne and I were struggling with our arithmetic assignment.

After a while Marianne said, "I just can't get this junk."

Elsie stopped reading. "I'll show you how if you want me to."

"I sure do," Marianne agreed.

I pretended to be working while I listened to Elsie explain the problems to Marianne. She certainly could teach better than my mother. Elsie turned my way and offered to help me, too.

"I don't need a thief helping me," I told her.

Marianne leaned over toward me. "Jenny, you could forget about that."

"Do *you* want to forget about it?" I asked. "She owes you a lunch. Elsie, when are you going to pay everyone back?"

"When I get the money," Elsie replied.

"What about your allowance?"

"I don't get any," Elsie said.

"I bet."

"You really don't get an allowance?" Marianne asked.

"No, I don't," Elsie answered.

"You just sit and stuff your mouth," I put in.

"Ohh," Marianne murmured.

The rest of the time in the library, Elsie kept her nose in her library book and pulled on her hair. I still couldn't do the fractions.

Mrs. Hanson took us to gym three days a week. But on Tuesdays and Fridays Mr. Marshall, the school P.E. teacher, took us. It was a lot more fun with Mr. Marshall. To make us eager to come to P.E., Mr. Marshall usually told us about the next week's lesson. But when he announced we were going to start folk dancing, we weren't eager. Some of the boys complained about being made to dance.

"You'll love it," Mr. Marshall told them. "You'll love it. How do you think a running back learns to make those swivel turns?"

The boys were not convinced.

Whenever we choose sides for baseball or basketball, the good athletes and the popular kids are chosen first. The kids who can't throw a ball have to stand around for last picks. When we chose partners for square dancing, you can imagine where that left Elsie.

"Come on, Elsie," Mr. Marshall said cheerfully, "you be my partner." He never let her get out of P.E. like Mrs. Hanson did.

First Mr. Marshall taught us to Allemande left. Then he told us to watch Elsie and him do a do-si-do. Mr. Marshall is very tall, and when Elsie skipped toward him she looked like a beachball rolling toward a flagpole. Jack and Lester laughed so hard they fell down. Mr. Marshall stopped everything.

"Jack," Mr. Marshall said, "do you like people to laugh at you?"

"No," Jack said.

"Lester," Mr. Marshall said, "do you like people to laugh at you?"

"I guess not," Lester said.

"Don't you know?"

"Yes . . . no, I don't like it." Lester fumbled around with his belt.

"Look at me, Lester, Jack."

The boys looked at him.

"If you don't like people to laugh at you, then don't you make fun of other people."

We went on with the folk dancing. Elsie still looked ridiculous, and plenty miserable, but no one dared laugh.

We did folk dancing for three weeks. I guess Elsie's diet was finally working. She didn't have much choice except to keep to it. Unfortunately, her mother didn't buy her new clothes or fix the old ones. While she danced, she kept hitching up her pants. When she bowed to her partner, her blouse went up and her pants slipped down, showing her blubbery back. Jack said she looked like a hog ready for slaughter. But he only said that when we got back to Mrs. Hanson's room.

Mrs. Hanson worked on our report cards at her desk. It was March and about that time again. I was worried. I knew I couldn't even get a C in arithmetic because of fractions. I'd never had a bad report card before.

The morning of the day report cards came out, Mrs. Hanson called each of us to her desk. She wanted us to look at the report card and discuss it with her if we didn't think it was fair. If some kid complained, Mrs. Hanson wrote down all his scores and asked him to average them. No one objected to a grade unless it was a real mistake. Nobody wanted to do all that math for nothing.

When I got called up to her desk, I was scared but still hoping for a miracle. I didn't get a miracle. I got a D minus. Two A's, three B's, and a lousy D minus. Diane wrote a note asking me what I got.

Elsie was the next one called up. I didn't really see what happened. I was too busy writing a note back to Diane, telling her I was going to get killed when I got home. What jerked me out of my note writing were the yells and laughter and Mrs. Hanson saying over and over, "May I please have your attention? May I please have your attention!"

I looked to the front of the room and saw Elsie

frantically pulling up her skirt over her white underpants. I poked Roy in the back. "What's going on? This some kind of striptease?"

Roy could only shake his head. He was laughing so hard tears wobbled in his eyes.

I turned to Diane. "What's going on?"

"When Elsie stood up, her skirt fell off," Diane answered me.

And then Jack let out a whoop.

This did it for Mrs. Hanson. She got her P.E. whistle out of her desk and blew it sharply. The room quieted.

"That is absolutely enough! I am ashamed of this class. Elsie . . ."

But it was too late to say anything to Elsie. She bunched the top of her skirt with one hand and pulled the classroom door open with the other. The door slammed behind her.

"Take out your arithmetic books and do page 360," Mrs. Hanson ordered. Page 360 was in the back of the book with solid pages of exercises.

"The whole page?" Roy asked.

"The whole page," Mrs. Hanson said firmly.

Slowly we all took out our books and paper and pencils. Diane stared at Mrs. Hanson hatefully. "She just likes to see us work."

"For talking, you may do page 360 *and* page 361, Diane," Mrs. Hanson told her.

I could see Diane draw air into her chest, getting ready to object, but the cross look on Mrs. Hanson's face changed her mind.

Page 360 was solid multiplication. Two numbers times four numbers. It was going to take all day. I hadn't even seen what happened, and I had to do forty-two problems. Mrs. Hanson gave me a pain. When I was on problem 3, she tapped me on the shoulder.

"Jenifer, will you please go to the girls' lavatory and see if Elsie is all right," she whispered to me.

Elsie was slumped against the wall at the end of the sinks. Her head was tipped back and her face tilted up. Tears were streaming from her eyes, but she didn't bother to brush them away. One hand hung at her side. The other still clutched her skirt. She looked sad and hopeless and alone.

I had never thought of Elsie as a human being. Just a fat girl.

"Are you O.K.?" I asked her. "Mrs. Hanson wanted me to see if you're O.K."

Elsie closed her eyes. The tears dripped from under her eyelids.

I stood there for a while. "I'll go get a safety pin from Mrs. Hanson so you can pin up your skirt."

Elsie didn't answer.

The classroom was silent. Everyone's head was bent

over an arithmetic book. I tiptoed up to Mrs. Hanson's desk.

"Can I have a safety pin for Elsie's skirt?"

"Certainly," she said and messed around in her top drawer until she found one.

When I returned to Elsie, she still had her eyes closed. I held out the pin. "Here. You can fix your skirt."

Elsie didn't seem to hear. She slid down the wall to the floor and sat there in a huge lump, her head drooping over her lap, tears falling onto her skirt.

I went into one of the stalls, came out, and fiddled with my hair in the mirror. She was still crying. I sat down on the floor beside her. "Elsie, it isn't that bad."

"What do you care?" she asked.

"Well, I don't want to see you cry."

"Then get out of here."

"No. Hey, Elsie, come on. Let's fix your skirt." I reached for her hand.

She pulled it away. "What do you care, Jenifer? Everyone likes you."

"Some people like you, too."

"Who?"

"Well . . . your mother and your sister and your friends."

"Not my mother, not my sister, and I don't have any friends." Elsie wiped her nose with her arm.

I got her a paper towel. "Somebody liked you once."

"No, they didn't. One person. Once my daddy did. That was five years ago."

I searched around in my head for something encouraging. "The kids will forget about this in a couple of days."

"So what?" Elsie's tears started coming again. "They all hate me. You hate me, too."

"No, I don't, Elsie. I did, but I don't now. I guess I didn't think about your having feelings."

Elsie's mouth drooped down on both sides. She stared ahead of her at the stall doors. I couldn't think of anything more to say. There was no point in trying to lie to her and say all the kids would learn to like her. Because they didn't and they wouldn't and she knew it.

Elsie heaved a shuddering sigh. "None of it matters anyway. I'll only be at this school a couple more months."

"Is your family moving away?"

"No, *I* am."

"How come?"

"Because the principal said I could just stay till the end of the school year on probation, and my mother doesn't want me anyway so she's sending me to a boarding school next fall."

"Maybe if you're good she'll change her mind."

"No, she won't. She wrote for all the boarding school

pamphlets after I got caught with the licorice whips."

"She could still change her mind."

Elsie didn't bother to answer. We sat there beside each other, silently.

"Elsie," I said, "I'll be your friend."

She turned her head slowly to look at me. "What for?"

"Because I want to."

"Why do you want a thief for a friend? Why do you want a fat slob who sits and stuffs her face?"

"I'm sorry I said those things. Can we be friends?" I smiled cheerfully at her.

She did not smile back. "As soon as you stop feeling sorry for me, you won't want to be seen with me."

"Are you girls all right?" It was Mrs. Hanson at the door.

I scrambled up. Elsie lugged herself up, holding onto her skirt.

"Here, Jenifer," Mrs. Hanson said briskly, "give me the pin and I'll fix Elsie's skirt. You go on back to class."

I felt things were unfinished between us so I lingered a minute, but Mrs. Hanson turned her back on me and started pinning Elsie's waistband.

At recess the kids clotted up into groups and began going over Elsie. I noticed Marianne back off toward the tetherball and start swinging it by herself. She was the only one who cared about Elsie's feelings.

"Why are we all standing around raking over Elsie?" I demanded. "What's so interesting about this?"

Sharon looked at me, surprised. "Skirts don't fall off every day in school, you know, Jenny."

"Well, how would you like yours to fall off? How would you like the whole class laughing at you?"

"I don't spend all my time eating," Sharon told me.

"Her skirt didn't fall off because she was eating," I informed Sharon. "It fell off because she wasn't eating."

"You mean because she *couldn't* eat," Diane put in.

"That's right," I said. "She gets jailed in the office every recess . . . for the whole semester! I never heard of anyone getting punished that long. Did you ever hear of anyone getting punished that long in this school, Sharon?"

"I never heard of anyone stealing so much." Sharon was getting mad.

"O.K., so she did. She can change. I remember you wet the bed in third grade and you were afraid of sleeping over at Diane's house. Do you still wet the bed, Sharon?"

Sharon's face turned bright pink. Her nostrils turned white. She was really mad now. I stalked over to the tetherball and asked Marianne if she wanted to play.

I felt bad the rest of the day. I didn't want to fight with my friends. I didn't want Sharon to be mad. I didn't want to take that report card home. I watched Elsie sitting at her desk reading and yanking on her hair. It was an ugly, ugly day!

The Tutor

I went in the front door, put my report card on the coffee table, and headed upstairs to my bed.

"That you, Jenny?" Mother called.

I kept going.

Mother came up after me. "What's the matter?"

"Nothing." My face was in my pillow. "I want to be left alone. Is that O.K.?"

"Where's your report card?"

"It's on the coffee table. Close the door. You can scream at me at dinner."

Mother left.

At dinner Daddy served me. "Having a little trouble with math, eh?" he asked.

"That's right. I'm stupid!"

Daddy put down his fork.

"We'll discuss the report card after dinner," Mother said hurriedly. "Kenny, do you want some peas?"

"What for? I got peas."

After dinner I stacked the dishes in the dishwasher and then went into the living room to sit down on the davenport.

Daddy looked over his paper. "What's the trouble with math?"

"I can't do fractions." A quaky feeling stirred inside me that meant I was going to cry.

"Don't you understand the problems when Mrs. Hanson explains them?" Mother asked.

I blinked my eyes fast. "No."

"Do you tell her when you don't understand?" Daddy asked.

"No."

"It seems to me that's the first thing to do, isn't it?"

"It wouldn't do any good. She just explains it again the same way. I don't . . ." My throat stuck. I couldn't get any more words out. I sat there blinking my eyes, but the tears came anyway.

"Jenny," Mother said, "we're not scolding you. We're trying to help you."

All I could do was shrug my shoulders.

"You'd better get her a tutor," Daddy said.

Mother sighed.

"Can I go to bed?" I asked.

"You might as well," Mother said.

She came up before I was asleep. I made room for her to sit on the edge of my bed.

"Maybe you do need a tutor. What do you think, Jenny?"

"I thought you and Daddy didn't have enough money."

"Well, we can always arrange money for important things."

Money. Math. Elsie. I sat straight up with the perfect solution. "Mother, Elsie can tutor me! She's way better than Mrs. Hanson or you. You won't have to pay her very much, and she needs the money to pay back what she stole."

"We weren't thinking of just helping, Jenny. We were thinking of hiring a real tutor, maybe a retired teacher."

"But, Mother, I'm not that bad. I just don't get fractions. Elsie gets one hundred every time. All I need is help for a few weeks. We go on to decimals next month."

"I don't think . . ."

"Mother, you could pay her fifty cents an hour, and

she could help me an hour every day. You could afford that, couldn't you? She'll know what the assignment is and just how to teach me."

"Jenny, I thought you didn't like Elsie. Why do you want her all of a sudden?"

"She's not so bad. You said yourself she had problems. Mother, why don't we try Elsie until the next test? Then if I don't pass the test, you can get a real teacher."

"Hmm, I guess that's possible—if Elsie wants to." Mother kissed me good night.

I flopped back on my pillow. I was satisfied with myself. Then, before I could get to sleep, doubts crept in. Sharon was still mad at me. What would she say if I brought Elsie home? I didn't want the kids to hate me. I wasn't as popular as Diane. What if I got stuck with Elsie as my only friend? I remembered Elsie saying when I got over being sorry for her I wouldn't want to be seen with her.

I decided that the best thing to do was to tell Diane what had happened in the girls' bathroom. If she started to feel sorry for Elsie, maybe she'd be on my side. In the morning I'd stop at Diane's house early so she'd be sure to walk with me, and then I could tell her.

That's just what I did. It looked like rain, so I hurried even faster than I'd planned. I got to Diane's before she'd finished her boiled eggs and soy-bread toast. Diane's mother is into nutrition. I sat down at the kitchen table and started right in with my story. I was lucky Diane was sort of sleepy. That way she listened instead of talked.

Diane's mother listened, too. "I remember after Jim died I got fat," she said slowly. "Every time I felt lonely, I went to the refrigerator."

Diane perked up. "I remember that, too. You got real porky."

"Maybe if you girls were friends with Elsie, she wouldn't have to eat all the time," Diane's mother suggested.

"She's good in math," I put in. "My mother was going to get me a tutor, but I got her to agree to pay Elsie to help me with fractions."

"You could use some help, too," Diane's mother told her. "Why don't you all work together?"

Diane didn't answer. She went for her coat. I waited on the porch. Everything had worked O.K. with her mother, but Diane hadn't said much. Sharon came up the walk. She stopped when she saw me.

"Hi," I said. "I'm sorry I was so crabby yesterday. Elsie was crying all over the bathroom and I felt sorry for her."

Sharon stood stiffly in her pink plastic raincoat. "That was really embarrassing for me to have the whole school know I used to wet the bed. My mother said a real friend would never tell that to anyone."

I walked down the porch steps. "I never told anyone before. I got a D minus on my report card in arithmetic. I was just all unglued yesterday."

"D minus!" That interested Sharon. "What did your parents do?"

"They said I should get a tutor." I didn't add the part about Elsie. I wanted to wait until Sharon and I were good friends again.

Diane came out the door. She was wearing the new blue spring coat her grandma had made for her, and she carried an umbrella. You can never trust it not to rain in the Northwest where we live. As we started off to school, Sharon moved to walk on one side of Diane. I had to walk on the other. Sharon wasn't ready to be good friends yet.

I was glad Elsie couldn't go out for recess. I had time to play with Diane and Sharon just as if nothing had happened. Sharon didn't talk to me as much as usual, but she didn't not play with me, either.

In P.E. I got a chance to ask Elsie about the tutoring. We were in line for our ups in a baseball game. She said she would have to ask her mother first before she could come over to my house. She said her mother would probably call my mother because her mother checked up on everything.

I invited Diane and Sharon over to my house after school. I hoped that would be O.K. with my mother. It was. She had baked cookies and she let us take some up to my room. Eating chocolate chip cookies and listening to my records thawed out Sharon.

While I was changing records, Diane suddenly asked, "Is Elsie really going to tutor you in arithmetic?"

"I don't know," I told her. "She has to ask her mother."

"How much are you going to pay her?"

"I think Mom will pay her fifty cents an hour."

"How long will she work each day?" Diane was sitting on my bed, looking at me intently. Sharon was sitting on the floor, sorting through records.

"I guess about an hour," I replied.

"At fifty cents an hour," Diane figured, "she can pay everybody back in a week. Maybe your mother should give us the money until she gets her debts paid."

"No, Diane, she'll pay everyone back. She doesn't like the kids to hate her."

"Why doesn't she act like it then?" Diane got up and opened my closet door. "Let me try on the housecoat you got for your birthday."

Sharon looked up. "How come Elsie's going to teach you?"

"Because she's cheaper than a real teacher," I told her.

"Oh," Sharon said. She handed me a record. "Play the Bee Gees."

I played the Bee Gees. Everything was going to be all right, I thought. I'd keep my friends, learn fractions, and Elsie would get skinny.

It didn't turn out to be quite that easy.

Money's Gone Again

Elsie's mother called my mother after dinner. I left the dishes and stood around the living room to listen. My mother can be very sweet to people. She was extra sweet to Mrs. Edwards, explaining how I had had the flu and had gotten behind, and since Elsie was so good in arithmetic, could she just come over after school for a few weeks to help me catch up? I didn't hear Mrs. Edwards' reply, but Mother widened her green eyes, laughed her phony laugh, and said, "Oh, heavens, of course you do. I only want to give Elsie a little tangible thanks for her kindness."

When Mother hung up, I asked, "What's tangible?"

"Something you can touch. Like money."

"Is Elsie's mother going to let her come?"

"Reluctantly. She wanted to be sure I know they have plenty of money, so it wouldn't be necessary to pay Elsie."

"She probably doesn't want to admit she can't trust Elsie with money."

"Jenifer," Mother said, "you'd better make it clear to Elsie that she pays her debts back first."

"I will," I promised. "Diane will kill her if she doesn't."

Mother needn't have worried. Each day Elsie went up to one of the kids she'd ripped off, said she was sorry, and handed over the money. Luckily, she paid Diane back first.

Elsie and I tried working on our dining room table, but Kenny was so fascinated by Elsie that he kept standing around staring at her. Elsie pretended she didn't notice. She was quite businesslike about teaching me. She carefully explained the steps I was to go through to do each problem and then had me do it. If I started to make a mistake, she stopped me immediately. She carefully explained again, did a problem just like it for me, and then had me start over. My whole assignment was finished in less than an hour.

After Elsie left, I asked Mother if she could keep

Kenny out of the dining room while we worked because it was embarrassing the way he stared at Elsie.

"I can hardly blame him," Mother answered. "She's the fattest little girl I've ever seen."

"She's lost a lot of weight," I said.

"Lost a lot of weight! How much did she weigh before?"

"I don't know, but now you can see her eyes. Before, they were all squished up. Anyway, Mother, can you keep Kenny away?"

"I'll try," Mother said.

She didn't try hard enough. When Elsie and I got to my house the next day, Kenny was playing with his Tonka truck in the kitchen. Before we had two problems finished, the dining room door opened and Kenny came through, crawling on his knees, pushing his truck ahead of him.

"Kenny, get out of here!" I ordered.

"It's my house," Kenny mumbled into the top of his truck.

"That's O.K. We're in here. You go into *your* kitchen."

Kenny continued around the dining room rug.

"Mo-ther!" I yelled.

Mother came to the door. "Come on, Kenny. You play in the kitchen with me."

"I don't want to," he said.

"Well, come on anyway." She leaned down to pick him up. Kenny scooted himself and his truck out of reach.

"Come with me, Kenny," Mother coaxed. "You're bothering the girls."

"No, I'm not," Kenny said and moved under the table.

"Oh, Mother, he's taking up the whole hour," I told her impatiently. She lets him get away with anything.

"Help me get him out then," she said.

Good! I reached under the table, grabbed him by an ankle, and shoved him toward Mother.

Kenny started to bawl. Mother picked him up. "Really, Jenifer, that wasn't necessary."

"You've got him, haven't you?" I sat down to start another problem as Mother carried Kenny out the door. Elsie hadn't said a word.

"He's spoiled," I told her.

"So's my little sister," Elsie replied.

A big howl came from the kitchen. Mother hurried through the dining room door, pulled the truck from under the table, and hurried back to the kitchen. The howling stopped.

"How old's your sister?" I asked Elsie.

"She's seven. How old's Kenny?"

"He's three and a half. He acts like he's two."

"All my sister has to do is cuddle up to my mother

and tell her she's pretty and she gets anything she wants and I get nothing."

"Why don't *you* tell your mother she's pretty?"

Elsie put her chin, or chins, on her hand. "I tried once. I told her that the blue dress she had on made her eyes look bluer. She snapped back at me that the sweater I was wearing made me look fatter and to go change it."

"That was mean!" It was so mean it made me feel bad. I guess it made Elsie feel bad, too. She sat up straight.

"Let's get your problems done," she said.

Every day for a week I got one hundred in arithmetic. The day before the test I was confident I would pass it. Mrs. Hanson reviewed fractions for us. I understood everything she said. If I started to get mixed up in the dividing and multiplying, I would think of Elsie's advice, "In multiplication, multiply across the top and multiply across the bottom. In division, turn the second fraction upside down and then multiply across the top and multiply across the bottom."

After math Mrs. Hanson let us choose groups to work on first aid skits for health. I got to choose a group, and I chose Sharon, Diane, and Elsie. No one acted like it was any big thing that I chose Elsie. Our group decided to do a skit on cuts. Diane was the girl

who cut her arm going through a sliding glass door.
Sharon was the owner of the house with the door. I
was the friend of the girl who cut her arm. Elsie was
the nurse in the doctor's office.

I thought our skit was the best in the class. Mrs.
Hanson must have thought so, too, because she gave
us all A's. She said Diane's acting was excellent, that I
knew the proper pressure points in giving first aid, that
Sharon was correct in hurrying the patient to the doctor, and that Elsie made an efficient nurse. It was a
nice day.

It was a nice day until Mrs. Hanson couldn't find the
Scholastic Book Club money. She was scrabbling
around at her desk during reading. I looked up several
times, wondering what she was doing. Finally she interrupted the class. "Did anyone see a large manila envelope on my desk?"

No one answered.

"It was right here this morning. It looks like this."
She held up a yellow envelope about the size of a piece
of school paper.

"What was in it?" Jack asked.

"All the book money you students turned in. I was
going to mail the order today, and I'm ready to count
the money. The envelope was right here on my desk
this morning. Does anyone remember seeing it?"

"Elsie sat at your desk when she was playing nurse,"
Jack said.

My heart thumped. My heart really, really thumped.

"Elsie, did you see the envelope on my desk?"

"No, I didn't," Elsie answered.

The room was quiet.

She wouldn't take it, I thought to myself. How could she have gotten it back to her desk?

Mrs. Hanson stood there thinking. She obviously didn't know what to do.

"I didn't take the money," Elsie announced loudly.

"Sure you didn't," Jack said.

"That isn't necessary, Jack," Mrs. Hanson told him. "I'll look some more after school. Take out papers for your spelling test."

Mrs. Hanson asked Elsie to stay a minute after the class was dismissed. I told Diane and Sharon to go on without me. Diane said O.K. and started walking. Sharon stopped to tell me I'd better get another tutor. I waited outside the classroom until Elsie came out. Her eyes looked sad. Her mouth was drooping down again.

"What did Mrs. Hanson say?" I asked as we left the building.

"She made me take everything out of my desk, and she felt through my clothes. Listen, I don't feel like tutoring today."

"Oh, that's O.K.," I said.

Elsie turned in the direction of her house. As she walked away, I saw her poking a finger into her hair, getting ready to yank on a curl. Mean things happen to Elsie. It isn't fair.

I tried to do my math in the dining room when I got home. I got all mixed up trying to cancel. I scrunched up my paper. Mother came in with diet pops.

"Where's Elsie?" she asked.

"She went home," I said.

"Jenifer, did you and Elsie have a fight?"

"No. She just didn't feel like tutoring today."

She started to hand me one of the cans of pop. Then she pulled it back. "Wait a minute. You don't need diet soda if Elsie isn't here. Go get a glass of milk."

"I don't want milk." I gathered up my book and papers and went up to my room. I wandered around my room, thinking. She just wouldn't take the money now. If she did, she was doomed in that classroom. She was doomed in the school, too. Mr. Douglas would probably kick her out.

At dinner Daddy told me there was a Bill Cosby special on TV.

"I can't watch TV tonight," I said.

"How come?" Daddy seemed disappointed. He and I like a lot of the same programs.

"I haven't finished my math, and we have a test tomorrow."

"What happened to your fat friend?"

"She couldn't tutor today. And I don't think it's very nice to say 'fat friend.'"

"Are you sure you didn't have a fight with her?"
Mother asked.

"No, I didn't have a fight with her, Mother."

"It seems too bad she couldn't come before a test,"
Mother said. "Well, we'll see tomorrow if you're caught
up with fractions."

I swallowed my bite of meat loaf. "You can't expect
me to get caught up in a week. That isn't fair."

"I didn't mean that you'd get an A. But don't you
think you can pass the test?" Mother wiped Kenny's
mouth with her napkin. He's old enough to wipe his
own mouth.

He pushed her hand away. There was still a smear
of tomato sauce on his upper lip. She wet her napkin
in her water glass and went at him again. Kenny
clamped down on her fingers with his teeth. Mother
yelped and pulled her hand away.

I laughed.

"Jenifer, that isn't funny!" Mother took Kenny off
his chair, swatted his bottom, and told him to go to
bed.

"Can't blame him," Daddy said when Kenny was
gone. "You should let him wipe his own mouth."

"Is that any excuse for biting me? If the children are
dirty, you criticize me. If I try to keep them clean, you
criticize me."

"I wasn't criticizing you. I was only . . ."

I left the table. I didn't need to hear the rest. I put

Elton John on my record player. I sat in the middle of my bed with my arithmetic book and papers. The part I hated was changing mixed numbers to improper fractions before multiplying. I kept thinking of Elsie. If she hadn't taken the envelope, she must be feeling awful right now.

Kenny pushed open my door. He had on his yellow pajamas with airplanes printed on them. He padded to my bed.

"I didn't get any dessert, Jenny." His mouth turned down like Elsie's.

I pulled him up on the bed beside me. "I didn't get any dessert, either."

He looked up in my face. "Were you bad, too?"

"No, I left the table before Mother served it."

"Don't you feel good? I don't feel good."

I cuddled him close to me. "I guess I don't feel so good." I rested my chin in his soft brown hair. He wasn't such a bad little brother.

When I got to school the next morning, Elsie was reading a library book.

"Hi," I said as I sat down at my desk.

She kept reading.

I didn't want to make a big show of talking to her. Yet I didn't want her to think I wasn't still her friend. I didn't know what to do.

Mrs. Hanson stood at the front of the room waiting

for our attention. "Students, I have a confession to make. You have a rather dumb teacher."

"No kidding," Diane said under her breath.

"It turns out," Mrs. Hanson went on, "that I didn't lose the book money after all. I thought I had left it on my desk, but when I went to the faculty room after school it was on the table there. Then I remembered I had taken it to the faculty room before school yesterday to count the money and give it to the secretary so she could give me a check to mail. I got talking to Mr. Douglas and forgot all about it."

I looked at Elsie. Her face was stony. I expected Mrs. Hanson to apologize to Elsie next. She didn't.

She said, "Take out your social studies books. We'll have the arithmetic test after recess."

"That was mean," I told Diane and Sharon at recess. "She made Elsie stay after school yesterday and searched her desk and searched all over her and then she didn't even apologize."

"Well, you can't blame her for thinking Elsie did it," Sharon said.

"Come on," Diane said. "Let's get in the baseball game." Diane was the best hitter among the girls. She always liked to play. I still wanted to talk about Elsie, but I guess no one else did.

While Mrs. Hanson passed out the test papers, I chewed my fingernails. I leaned over to Elsie.

"I'm not sure about cancellation," I whispered.

"Don't do it," Elsie whispered back. "You can multiply without canceling."

When you don't cancel you have to multiply and divide with bigger numbers. I was the last one to hand in my test. All the other kids were reading their library books. No one was allowed to talk or move around until everyone had finished.

Mrs. Hanson corrected our papers while we were at P.E. with Mr. Marshall. Just before school ended, she passed them out. I got a B minus, Elsie got an A, Sharon got a C, and Diane got a C minus. We weren't supposed to discuss our grades. They were nobody's business but our own, Mrs. Hanson said. We did anyway.

On the way home Elsie didn't even talk about her A. I was crowing about my B minus so much that Diane finally told me to shut up—a B minus wasn't that great.

Mother thought it was, though. She beamed at the paper, she beamed at me, and she beamed at Elsie. "Elsie, you're marvelous," my mother told her, sitting down at the dining room table with us. "You're absolutely marvelous. When I try to teach Jenny, I mix her up worse." Mother pushed her chair back. "Come on. Dad's working tonight. I'll take us all to the Dairy Queen for sundaes."

Elsie stayed seated. "Thank you, Mrs. Sawyer, but I can't go. I'm on a diet."

"Oh, my goodness, I forgot. I'm sorry, dear." Mother put her hand on Elsie's shoulder. "You've been so good about it, too. It must be hard. I'll think of some way to celebrate."

It was sort of stupid of Mother to forget Elsie's diet. I could see why she did, though. The more I knew Elsie the more I forgot she was fat. She had the prettiest teeth when she smiled, which wasn't very often.

Mother went humming happily out of the room, taking my paper with her.

"You have a nice mother," Elsie said.

"She is most of the time," I agreed. "Sometimes she gets crabby."

"You're lucky. Mine's crabby all the time. At least to me."

Mrs. Hanson didn't give homework on test days. It was raining so we decided to go up to my room to listen to records. I got out my pile of records and Elsie sat down on the bed with me. The bed creaked under her weight.

"Don't you have any Rolling Stones?" she asked, going through the pile.

"No, do you?"

"I don't. But my mother does. I listen to them when she goes out. I like that one, 'As Tears Go By.' " Elsie tilted her head back and sang.

I was amazed. "Elsie, you sound like a real singer. Where did you learn to do that?"

"My sister and I practice singing along with Mother's records when we're home alone."

"Does she leave you alone much?"

"Yeah, she's got a new boyfriend."

"Is he neat?"

"He's O.K., I guess. I haven't seen him much. He's got a Porsche, and Mama likes that."

"We've got an eleven-year-old Volkswagen, and my mother doesn't like that," I said.

Elsie laughed. Then her face drooped into its sad lines again. "I wish we could keep on going to school together."

"We probably can," I said. "If you're real good at school and keep on your diet, the principal and your mother will probably change their minds."

"Maybe," Elsie said, looking down at my bed and picking at the yellow yarn in my quilt.

"Sure they will. If you're good," I insisted. I really believed that then. Sometimes my mother'd get mad at me or crabby, and sometimes I thought she loved Kenny more. Sometimes she might even scream at me, but I always knew she wanted me.

Elsie was still looking sadly at my bed, and I was trying to think of something else to convince her we'd keep on going to school together, when Kenny pushed open my bedroom door with Mother behind him. Mother had that happy, bustling look she gets around Christmas and birthdays.

"Get your coats on, girls. We're going shopping," she announced.

"I think it's about time for me to be going home." Elsie got up off the bed and the mattress sprang back up.

"No, no," Mother corrected her. "First we're going shopping and then I'll drive you home. We're going to get a present for each of you."

"Me, too," said Kenny.

"No, you didn't get a B or an A on a test today," Mother told him.

"I didn't have a test," Kenny said.

"You're too little to have a test. You only get tests when you go to school. Come on, girls. Let's go." Mother waved us toward the door.

Kenny took my hand. "You'll give me a test. Won't you, Jenny?"

"We'll give you a test in the car," I promised him.

Elsie and I sat in the back seat. Kenny sat in front with Mother. He peeked at us through the two front seats.

"Give me my test now, Jenny," he demanded.

"O.K.," I said, "count to ten."

Kenny counted, "One, two, three, four, five, six, eight, nine, ten!"

"You only get a B," I said. "You missed number seven."

"Oh!" Kenny started to cry.

"Don't worry. Don't worry, a B gets you a present," I assured him.

Kenny peeked through the crack in the seats again. "You give me a test, Elsie."

Elsie's sad mood seemed to drop away. She licked her upper lip in thought. "All right, here's your test. What color is Jenny's sweater?"

"Yellow," Kenny said.

"Right," Elsie said.

"I got it right, Mama."

Mother was trying to park in the shopping center evening traffic. "Umm-hmm, dear," she murmured as she turned the wheel hard to squeeze the car into a small space.

"Give me another test, Elsie."

"What color is your mother's coat?"

"Red!" Kenny shouted.

"Right!" Elsie shouted back. "You get an A."

"I got an A, Mama! I got an A, Mama," Kenny kept yelling as we piled out of the car.

"Yes, dear." She took his hand. "Where do you girls want to go?"

"Where can we go?" We had stopped under the eaves in front of a line of stores.

"Let's see. Pay'n'Save or Woolworth's," Mother suggested.

"Pay'n'Save," I decided. "Can we both get a record?"

"I think that would be perfect." Mother led us into the store.

Elsie and I flipped through the bins of records while Kenny hopped up and down, telling Mother to get him a record, too. She picked out a Burl Ives for him. Elsie picked out a Rolling Stones record. I picked out an Elton John I didn't have.

Riding back to Elsie's house, I told Mother that Elsie could sing.

"Great!" Mother said. "Let's all sing 'I Know an Old Lady Who Swallowed a Fly.' "

We sang all the way to Elsie's, Kenny singing the wrong words in his tinny little voice. When Elsie got out with her record and thanked Mother, she was smiling all over, showing her pretty teeth and a dimple.

"She's a nice girl," Mother said as we drove away.

"You know how many people think so?" I asked Mother.

"How many?"

"Two. You and me."

The next day was Saturday and Mother was going for a job interview. She said she'd pay me to take care of Kenny, and besides, I could have a friend over for the afternoon. Diane was visiting her grandmother and Sharon was going shopping with her aunt, so I called Elsie. Elsie was stuck at home with her little sister, but she invited me to come over there. That was O.K. with

Mother. I was glad. I was very much interested to see what Elsie's house looked like inside.

Elsie's house was fancier than ours. There were tall vases on end tables and a blue cigarette box and a glass frog on the coffee table in the living room. I held Kenny's hand while we walked through.

Elsie led us out to the backyard. For once it was sunny. Most of the time it just rains. Kenny and Elsie's little sister took turns on the swing set. Elsie and I played checkers on the picnic table. Elsie beat me twice. I was so determined to win the third game I didn't notice how quiet it was in the yard until Elsie asked, "Where did Kenny and Robyn go?"

We found them in the kitchen having a graham cracker fight. Graham crackers were scrunched all over the kitchen floor.

"You clean up this mess before Mama gets home!" Elsie screamed at her little sister.

"Come on, Kenny, you help," I told him.

Elsie's little sister got out the broom and spattered crumbs around with it. "Gimme the broom," Elsie ordered. "You put the big pieces in the garbage bag."

I heard a car pull up in the driveway. Elsie froze, holding the broom still. Robyn ran out the back door.

Mrs. Edwards took one look at the mess in the kitchen, marched over to Elsie, yanked the broom from her hands, and smacked her across the bottom with it. "I can't trust you alone one hour, can I?"

I thought Mrs. Edwards should know it wasn't Elsie's fault. Elsie didn't explain so I started in. "It wasn't Elsie's fault, Mrs. Edwards. Kenny and . . ." My voice faded away.

Mrs. Edwards was looking right at me. Her face was stony cold. "Elsie won't be able to play any more today," she said. "I think you and your brother better run along home."

I glanced at Elsie, who was crouched on the floor picking up pieces of graham crackers. "I'll see you later, Elsie," I said. I grabbed Kenny's hand and got out of there.

"She's a mean mama," Kenny said as I hurried him on home.

She was. She was a lot meaner than I had thought.

The Slumber Party

When I stopped at Diane's house on the way to school Monday morning, her mother asked me, "What did you get on your arithmetic test?"

"B minus."

"B minus." Diane's mother turned to Diane at the kitchen table. "Did you know that?"

"Of course I knew that." Diane was drinking the last of her orange juice. She put the glass down. "What's the big deal about a B minus?"

"Jenny was sick for two weeks. You weren't. And you got a C minus."

Diane stood up. "So what? She's got Elsie to help her every day."

Diane's mother turned to me. I was standing by the door, waiting. "Jenny, why don't you bring Elsie over here after school today? Then, when you girls finish your lessons, I'll be home and we can plan Diane's slumber party."

"I guess so," I said. "But I'll have to ask my mother first."

"No problem. I'll call your mother this morning."

Diane grabbed her coat and pulled me out the door.

"Remember, Diane," her mother called after us, "you girls will come here after school."

"O.K., O.K., we heard you." Diane slammed the door behind us.

"What did you tell her you got a B minus for?" Diane asked as we started down the street.

"What was I supposed to tell her? Anyway, C's average."

"C is average. Not a C minus," Diane said in her mother's voice.

"You should have my mother," I said. "Average isn't good enough. She didn't go to college, so she's got it all planned for me."

We saw Sharon ahead of us. We raced to catch up with her.

On the way home from school, I told Elsie we were

going to Diane's house to study. We were walking slowly behind Sharon and Diane to keep them from hearing us. I explained to Elsie that Diane's mother doesn't get paid much on her job. She wants Diane to have everything other kids have, but she doesn't always have the money, so she drives us places and does a lot of favors to make up for it. "She can't pay you," I explained, "but she'll probably do something else for you."

"I don't care about the money," Elsie replied. "But doesn't Diane hate me?"

"I don't think she hates you any more," I said. "She doesn't stay mad long like Sharon. She's just sort of bossy. My mom says it's because she's been alone with her mother since her dad died. But I remember she was bossy way before that."

When we went into Diane's house, I could tell Elsie was still nervous because she hung back and left her coat on. Diane headed for the kitchen. I took Elsie's arm and pulled her along. We sat down at the table while Diane got us glasses of orange juice.

We sipped our juice. No one said anything. Finally I opened my book. "Let's get started. I have to be home in an hour."

"Me, too," Elsie said and opened her book.

Diane slowly opened hers. I could see her heart wasn't in this. I hoped she'd be nice.

"Why don't we do the first problem by ourselves and then we'll compare answers," I suggested.

Diana shrugged and began to work. Elsie, who was finished in about two seconds, sat and waited for us. Elsie's and my answers were the same. Diane's was different. Elsie leaned over and looked at Diane's paper.

"If you turn the second fraction upside down instead of the first one, you'll get it right," she said.

Diane did the problem again. She raised her eyebrow when she shoved her paper over to us, and her new answer was the same as ours. "You must be pretty smart," she told Elsie.

"As long as it's something I can do sitting down," Elsie answered matter-of-factly.

We did the rest of the page the same way. Toward the end Diane was catching on and we were all getting the same answers. Diane was in a good mood when we finished.

"Can you come to my slumber party Friday night?" she asked Elsie.

"Maybe," Elsie said. "I have to ask my mother. She'll probably call your mother."

"What are you on—parole?" Diane asked.

Elsie shrugged. "Just about."

When Diane's mother came home, she said it would be no problem about Elsie. She would call Mrs. Edwards herself, and she did. The phone was in the kitchen. We girls sat and listened.

Diane's mother mostly listened, too, except for saying over and over, "It isn't necessary for the girls to eat in order to have a good time." She let out a long sigh as she put the receiver back on the hook.

"Well? Can she come?" Diane asked.

"Yes, but Elsie has to come *after* dinner and go home *before* breakfast."

"No biggy," Diane said. "We won't be getting up till noon."

There were six of us at Diane's slumber party—Sharon, Elsie, Diane, Diane's two cousins, and me. Diane's younger cousin was in the third grade and sort of out of it. Her older cousin was in the eighth grade. All the older cousin wanted to do was talk about boys, which got pretty boring.

Diane put up with her telling about John, who let her ride his minibike, and Ed, who played guitar and was just darling. When she got to cute David, who helped her with English papers, Diane asked her if she had any lipstick in her purse. Diane's cousin had lipstick, mascara, an eyebrow pencil, an eyelash curler, and eye shadow. We had a ball! When Diane's mother came into Diane's bedroom with glasses of juice and popcorn, she said we looked like the chorus line at the Rivoli.

After she left, we put on our housecoats. Elsie's was

purple with a ruffle around the neck. I had a lampshade in my bedroom that had a ruffle on top, slanted
straight out, and a ruffle on the bottom. I thought Elsie
looked like my lampshade, but I wouldn't have told her
that.

Diane's mother had given five of us grape juice and
Elsie grape*fruit* juice. We took our glasses and sat in a
circle on the floor. Diane passed the popcorn. Elsie
didn't take any.

"Don't you get hungry?" Diane asked her.

"Not so much any more," Elsie said. "At first I did.
At first all I could think about was food. All I dreamed
about was food. I even thought of eating the plants in
my room one night."

"How'd you get so fat in the first place?" Diane's little
cousin asked.

"Well, I always used to be plump." Elsie started her
story. "Mama was, too. Daddy used to pinch our bot-
toms and say we were his cute little butter balls. Then
Daddy and Mama started to have trouble. They would
argue, Daddy would slam out of the house, and then
she'd yell at me. I got so if I heard them fighting I'd
get in my bed so she wouldn't have anything to yell at
me about." Elsie stopped and sipped her juice.

"Well, go on," Diane's little cousin said impatiently.
"How did you get fat?"

"Just gradually. Daddy started staying away. Mama

was busy with my sister because she was only two. No-body paid any attention to me. If I whined around Mama, she'd tell me to go get a cookie. It got so every time I felt sad I went to the kitchen and pulled down some cookies or graham crackers to eat. After a while I was eating all the time. There was nothing else to do."

"Didn't your dad come to take you places?" Diane's big cousin wanted to know. "Our folks are divorced and our dad takes us every other week."

"He did at first. Then they had a big fight and Mama said the judge gave my sister and me to her. Daddy just came a couple of times after that. I called him once at his office when I was eight. I was crying on the phone. That's when the kids at school started making fun of me. He said he'd come to see me on Sunday. He had a lady with him. They took me out to dinner. I remember she stared at me while I was gobbling down my food. When he took me back to my house, I think he started to say something about the next Sun-day, but I saw the lady shake her head. I haven't seen him since."

"Didn't your mother stop you from eating?" asked Sharon.

"She tried. But by then it was too late. She went on a diet and put me on one, too. But I'd just sneak food or steal food. She couldn't understand how she got thinner and I got fatter. She found out when my fourth grade teacher called her on the phone."

"Was she mad?" Diane's little cousin asked.

Elsie nodded. "She was real mad."

The popcorn bowl was empty. Diane went to her bedroom door and yelled for her mother. When she came up, Diane's mother looked around the room at our piles of clothes.

She picked up Elsie's blouse and pants and shook them out. "Diane, why don't you hang these things up?"

"They're not hurting anything," Diane told her. "Here, take the bowl."

Diane's mother looked closely at Elsie's pants. "What are all these pins?"

"Those are mine," Elsie said, getting up off the floor. "I have to pin them or they'll fall down. I'll hang them up."

"No, let me take in the seams on the sewing machine. I can do it in a minute."

Elsie reached for her clothes. "No, that's all right. The pins work."

Diane's mother held up her hand. "They'll look better sewn." She headed for the door with Elsie's pants.

"Here." Diane went after her. "Take the bowl."

Diane's mother took the bowl and the pants and went downstairs.

Elsie sat on the floor and opened her night case. "I've got something for everyone," she announced. She took out her clean underpants and socks and put them on the floor. In the bottom of the case were six small velveteen bags. Elsie walked around the room and gave one to each of us.

Diane's cousin put her little bag to her nose. "It's lavender. It smells yummy."

I smelled mine. It was lavender. The bag was brown with yellow flowers. It was tied with a long yellow ribbon. I noticed Sharon's was dark blue with pink flowers and pink ribbon. I thought mine was the prettiest. I guess Sharon was pleased with hers, though. Sharon is an extremely piggy person who likes to be given gifts, and she kept fingering the velveteen and rubbing the little bag on her cheek.

Suddenly she jumped up and went over to where Elsie was sitting, reached down, and hugged her. "Thank you, Elsie. We'll have a big party for you on your birthday."

Elsie bent her head down as she slowly put her pants and socks over the last bag in her case. "I won't be here on my next birthday."

"Why not?" Diane's little cousin wanted to know.

"I'll be at a boarding school."

Sharon stood over Elsie with her hands on her hips. "Why? Don't you like our school?"

"I like your school, but the principal doesn't like me."

"Oh, Mr. Douglas," Sharon scoffed and sat down beside Elsie. "He always acts strict, but after he punishes you, he forgets."

Elsie shook her head. "My mother won't forget."

"Sure, she will," Diane insisted.

"No, I stole in the other school, too. This was going to be my last chance, and I wrecked it."

"Does your mother always pick on you?" Diane's little cousin asked.

"She used to be real nice to me. That was before Daddy started staying away." Elsie's face looked dreamy. "She's a good sewer, too, and she made all our dresses alike. She told everyone I was her carbon copy. But then Daddy left and she got thinner and I got fatter and she never said that any more. Now she says I act just like Daddy if I complain about anything. I hate her when she screams at me, but when I hear her cry, I feel sad."

Sharon was bouncing around impatiently. Sharon isn't interested in how people feel. "Elsie, what boarding school will you go to?"

"I don't know." Elsie shrugged. "Mama's already got the pamphlets from three schools."

"All you have to do is be an eager beaver for the rest of the year," Diane explained in her bossy voice. "Just do the dishes for your mother, even when she doesn't ask you, and take out the garbage, and stuff. By June you'll have her all mellowed out."

Diane looked satisfied with herself. That would work with most mothers, but I wasn't sure about Mrs. Edwards. Elsie obviously didn't think so, either. She was sitting there all sagged down. I hurried and asked her where she got the little bags.

Elsie said her last year's teacher had taught her to make sachets for Christmas. Elsie picked the lavender and dried it in the summer. When she got the tutoring money, after she'd paid back what she owed us, she bought the velveteen. She told us how she'd pawed through the remnant pile in the fabric store to find the prettiest pieces. My mother grew lavender in her garden. I thought to myself I'd pick it and dry it the next summer, and then I'd have pretty gifts to give.

We didn't go to sleep until two-thirty. Diane's little cousin told a ghost story that was dumb. Then her big cousin told a ghost story that was scary. We were in our sleeping bags and had the lights out by then. Sharon wanted to turn the lights back on. Diane wouldn't. As I drifted off to sleep, I was glad I had brown hair and brown eyes like my dad. I didn't think he'd care if I got fat.

Diane's mother woke us up at ten because Elsie's mother had called and wanted her to come right home.

We stayed in our sleeping bags and watched Elsie get dressed. Her pants did look better not bunched up with pins.

I guess Elsie's mother didn't think so, though. We were all in the kitchen, eating, when she called.

We could hear her scream at Diane's mother, who was holding the receiver away from her ear. "If I want my child's clothes altered, I'll take care of it myself!"

"I certainly hope you do!" Diane's mother snapped back. "It's about time you paid attention to her!" Diane's mother slammed down the phone. She and Diane had a lot in common.

Daddies Don't Wear Aprons

Elsie wore a new green corduroy jumper to school on Monday. She had on new sandals, too. Ones that stayed on her feet. I wondered if her mother was so mad that she wouldn't let Elsie tutor any more. I guess she wasn't. Elsie tutored us at Diane's house or my house every day after school except on Friday.

My mother got a job at the EverBloom Nursery on Fridays and Saturdays. I would have to pick up Kenny at the neighbors' on Friday, take him home, and babysit. I didn't mind, because Mother said she'd pay me. Daddy minded. He wanted to know who was going to make dinner. Mother said she'd make an extra casserole on Thursday and I could put it in the oven for Friday's dinner.

"What about Saturday?" Daddy asked.

"Oh, you can shop for whatever you like to eat and you and Jenny can cook it."

"Would you like me to scrub the floors on my day off, too?"

"That would be nice." Mother laughed.

Daddy didn't. "What am I supposed to do about bowling?"

"You can shop in the morning and get dinner after you bowl." Then she added, "Our car isn't going to last much longer."

Daddy looked up. "What's that supposed to mean?"

"I mean," she said in the voice she uses with Kenny, "that unless I work we can't afford a new car."

"Thank you very much." Daddy got up and left the table.

"I don't think Daddy likes to cook," I said to Mother.

Her mouth was stretched into a thin line. "He'll learn," she said.

On Friday, I put the macaroni and cheese casserole in the oven. Kenny put the spoons, knives, and forks on the table, all in the wrong order. Daddy sat in the living room, waiting to be served, as usual. I added dishes of canned peaches because the table looked so bare. We had Oreo cookies for dessert.

When Mother came home, she said the dinner was lovely. She looked pooped. At bedtime she gave me an extra-long hug and told me I was a doll.

Saturday morning when I got up, Mother was gone. I waited around for Daddy to say something about shopping. He didn't. He was fiddling with his calculator, which wouldn't work. I got tired of playing with D.D., so finally I asked him if I could go over to Diane's. He said sure and to take Kenny with me.

"What am I going to do with him at Diane's?" I asked.

"Well, what am I going to do with him here?" Daddy asked back.

I dragged Kenny to Diane's. She wasn't pleased.

Daddy came back from bowling about five. He sat down in his big chair with the paper. At six Kenny began to whine.

"Aren't we going to have dinner?" I asked Daddy.

He folded his paper to look at his watch. "Your mother should be here pretty soon."

"No, she won't," I told him. "She called when you were bowling and said they were having a rose sale and she wouldn't get home until about seven."

"Oh, for . . ." He put down his paper, went into the kitchen, and started opening and closing cupboard doors. He piled cheese, mayonnaise, mustard, and butter on the counter. He sliced the cheese, I toasted the sandwiches, and Kenny set the table.

We were eating when Mother got home. While she took off her shoes, I made her a fresh, hot sandwich. She gave me a tired smile.

The next Saturday it dawned on me that I had a whole afternoon without a parent around. As soon as Daddy left for bowling, I spread a bunch of newspapers on the living room floor. I went down to the basement, found some scraps of wood, Daddy's hammer and nails, and brought them upstairs. I dumped the whole mess on the newspapers and told Kenny to go to it. He whacked away happily for an hour and fifteen minutes while I called up every friend I had.

We had toasted cheese sandwiches for dinner, again.

The following Saturday Elsie called me. She was stuck with her little sister for the day. I told her to come on over; I was stuck with Kenny. I phoned Diane and Sharon and asked them over, too.

First we drank up all the pop in the house. Then we went up to Mother's room to try on her earrings and shoes.

Diane flopped around on Mother's bed. "This is boring, staying in the house."

Elsie turned away from the mirror. Mother's amber earrings dangled down her plump neck. "There's a carnival in the shopping center," she said.

Sharon unbuckled Mother's high-heeled sandals. "I haven't got any money."

"I have," Elsie told her. "I saved all my tutoring money this week. I'll share it."

Diane bounced off the bed. "Neat-o! Let's go."

I made sure Kenny went to the bathroom before we started off to the carnival. Poor Elsie might have been better off if I hadn't. Maybe we would have turned back. But we didn't.

The Hitchhikers

We sang with Elsie down the first six blocks to the shopping center. Her little sister, Robyn, danced ahead of us, swinging her new red purse by the chain. It was the end of April, no clouds in the sky for a change. We walked the seventh block. We dragged down the eighth. I was carrying my sweater and Kenny's sweater. Pretty soon, I knew, I'd be carrying Kenny. We moved more and more slowly.

A flatbed truck came up the road. Diane hopped to the curb and put out her thumb. Elsie yelled, "No, Diane," and went after her.

The truck came to a halt. The driver leaned out of his cab. "Where are you kids headed?" He was a gray-haired man with greasy lines on his face.

Elsie backed away.

"We're going to the Lynnwood shopping center," Diane answered him.

"I'll be ending up there," he said. "Hop in the back."

We all clambered up on the flatbed except Elsie and her sister. Elsie yanked on her sister's sleeve. "Let's walk."

Her sister pulled away. "I'm tired of walking." She climbed in the truck.

Elsie still hung back.

"Get in, Fatty, or get off the curb," the driver yelled.

Diane put out her hand. "Come on, Elsie. We'll help you."

Reluctantly Elsie lugged herself up and squatted down with us.

As the truck lumbered down the street, Diane said to Elsie, "See, isn't this better than walking?"

Elsie held onto the slats on the side of the truck. "Bad things can happen to kids who hitch rides."

"I can run faster than that old man can," Elsie's sister said. She stood up to lean over the railing, leaving her purse on the truck floor.

"We'll get there in five minutes," Diane stated. "It would have taken an hour walking."

Five minutes passed. When ten minutes passed, Elsie's face pinched up with worry. I watched the buildings swish by. We weren't anywhere near the shopping center. I didn't want to seem chicken, but I was getting an uneasy feeling in my stomach. "It's taking a long time," I said.

Sharon looked out through the slats at the street. "We aren't even going the right way."

"He's probably got to do an errand first," Diane assured her. "He said he'd end up at the shopping center."

The truck rumbled on and on. This wasn't right at all.

"You'd better make him stop, Diane," Sharon said.

"Don't worry. He'll stop," Diane replied.

Elsie inched over to the cab's back window and rapped on the glass. The truck kept going.

"Diane, I'm scared." Sharon began to cry.

"Don't be a baby," Diane said. I noticed, though, that she had her finger in her mouth, pulling on her bottom teeth.

Elsie rapped on the cab window some more. It didn't do any good. She inched back to us. "We'd better jump."

"Are you crazy?" Diane demanded. "We'd break our legs."

I was thinking that Elsie wouldn't break her leg.

She'd just bounce off and roll. I snickered to myself.

"This isn't funny, Jenny," Sharon told me. "How are we going to get home?"

Kenny twisted around in my lap and put his hands up on the sides of my face. "Jenny, how are we going to get home?"

"I don't know, Kenny. How *are* we going to get home, Diane?" I asked.

Diane didn't answer. Her eyes were shifting from side to side. She was scared. The only one who wasn't scared was Elsie's sister. She was still leaning over the rail, waving to cars that passed by. I caught a glimpse of a street sign. The number was in the hundreds. The houses were getting farther apart. We were way out of town. I shivered with fear.

We sat there like dummies, not talking or moving. Kenny crouched in my lap, whimpering for Mama. I searched in my mind for an escape. If we tried to signal a car, the driver would just wave back, thinking we were friendly like Elsie's sister. We weren't passing any police cars. The truck was going too fast to jump. What could we do? I wasn't watching houses flash by now. I was watching trees. Sharon kept crying and rocking back and forth, bumping my legs. I didn't dare cry with Kenny in my lap.

"We'll wait for a red light and jump," Elsie said.

"What?" Diane said stupidly. "What red light?"

"There aren't any red lights out here," Sharon whined.

"There might be," Elsie said. "There might be at a highway or an intersection. I'll watch ahead. You get on the edge ready to jump."

Sharon, Diane, Kenny, and I crawled to the end of the truck and dangled our legs over the edge. Elsie lifted herself up by the slats to stand next to her sister. She tried to make Robyn sit down with us, but Robyn wouldn't. Elsie gave up and stuck her head over the railing to watch for a traffic light.

I held Kenny's hand tightly in mine while I banged my feet on the truck's license plate to entertain him. Every once in a while I'd look back at Elsie. She was staring straight ahead. When the sun went behind the trees, Kenny complained he was cold. I put on my sweater and helped Kenny with his.

"There's a light! There's a light!" Elsie yelled. "Get ready."

The truck slowed. I jumped off before it stopped. A car behind the truck screeched to a halt. The driver hollered out his window, "What do you kids think you're doing?"

I ignored him and lifted Kenny out. Sharon and Diane jumped down. Elsie came last, pulling her sister after her. Robyn was screaming, "My purse! My purse!"

"Forget your purse," Elsie told her. "Come on!"

But Robyn wouldn't forget her purse. She yanked loose from Elsie and scrambled back in the truck after it. Elsie tried to climb up to get her. The light must have changed because the truck lurched forward and Elsie fell to the ground.

The driver behind us blasted his horn and started coming. We scrambled out of the way. The truck went down the road with Elsie's sister still in the back. We huddled together on the side of the road, watching it disappear.

The Outcast

"Jenny, Jenny." Kenny pulled at my sweater. "Where are we, Jenny?"

"I don't know," I told him. There were no houses nearby. There was an old garage across the street and a tavern at the corner on our side of the road.

"We better call the police," Diane said.

I took Kenny's hand and we headed for the tavern. Diane and Sharon walked with me. Elsie stumbled after us. The tavern was dark inside. It smelled sour. I could see a man in a white apron behind the counter. Another man on a stool turned to stare at us.

"You kids can't come in here," the man with the apron said.

Diane pointed at Elsie, who was standing behind us, shaking. "Her sister's been kidnapped. We have to call the police."

"Who kidnapped her?" the man asked.

"A truck driver," Diane answered.

"A truck driver?"

"Yes, you see . . ." Diane walked up to the counter. The rest of us hung back at the door. "We were hitch-hiking and a man in a truck picked us up. Only he went the wrong way so we jumped out of the truck, but her sister's still in it."

"Where are you kids from?" the man wanted to know.

"We live in Brier."

"Brier! Where were you going?"

"To the Lynnwood shopping center."

"You're way out of your territory."

"I know. The truck driver went the wrong way and he's still got her sister." Diane pointed at Elsie again.

"You kids go sit in that booth. I'll get the police."

We slid onto the wooden benches in the booth. Elsie sat in the corner pulling on her hair. Tears dripped down her face.

"The police will get your sister, Elsie," I said.

Elsie shook her head.

"Sure they will," Sharon put in. She was feeling braver.

"Even if they do, Mama will be through with me."

"It isn't your fault your sister's dumb," Diane said. "You tried to get her out."

Elsie took a paper napkin out of the metal holder and blew her nose. "It doesn't matter. Mama won't keep me now."

"Your mother can't give you away," I said.

"She'll send me to boarding school and never bring me back."

"You aren't that bad," I said.

Elsie's face crumpled. "Yes, I am!" She put her head down on the table and sobbed.

I felt awful for her, but I didn't know how to make her feel better. I just sat there patting her back sort of helplessly.

After a while a tall policeman pushed open the tavern door. He looked at the man in the apron. The man in the apron was pouring beer. He nodded toward us. The policeman walked over to our booth. "Which one of you lost your sister?"

"She did." Diane pointed at Elsie. "We were hitchhiking . . ."

"You look old enough to know better than to hitchhike."

That rattled Diane for a minute. She took a big

breath before she went on with our story. Kenny didn't listen to Diane. He stared, popeyed, at the big gun in the policeman's belt.

When Diane finished, the policeman asked how old Elsie's sister was.

Elsie lifted her teary face. "My sister's seven," she whispered.

The policeman wanted to know what Elsie's sister looked like, what the truck driver looked like, what kind of truck he drove, and the truck's license number. I remembered I had kicked the license plate, but I hadn't thought of looking at it.

The policeman closed his tablet. "You kids wait here. I'll be back to get you in a minute." He went outside, leaving the tavern door open. We could hear him talking on his car radio, something about heading east, seven-year-old girl, blond hair.

When he came back he said he was going to give us a ride in his patrol car to the police station. Our parents could pick us up there. We were quiet in the back of the patrol car. Kenny whispered to me that he had to go to the bathroom. I whispered back that he'd have to wait.

Inside the police station the policeman left us standing at the counter while he disappeared through a door marked "No Admittance."

Kenny was wiggling beside me. I asked one of the

uniformed ladies at a desk behind the counter if she could tell me where the bathroom was. She said down the hall and to the right.

When Kenny and I got back from the bathroom, another policeman was standing at the counter writing down Sharon's name and phone number. After I gave him my name and phone number, he told us to wait on the bench for our parents. Elsie sat on the end of the bench. I held Kenny in my lap until he wriggled so much I let him down. He raced around the shiny floor. Every once in a while his feet slipped and he crashed into our legs.

Diane told him to cut it out when he landed on her. Elsie didn't complain. Her eyes were open, but I don't think she saw anything. I heard her sigh once in a while. I thought how awful it would be to be sent away.

Diane's mother was the first to come. She kissed Diane and then hugged all of us in turn. When she got to Elsie, Elsie looked up at her dumbly. I thought Elsie acted like an animal that has been run over. Diane's mother kept an arm around Elsie as she listened to the whole story. I noticed Diane left out the part where she stuck out her thumb for the truck to stop. When Diane finished, her mother went up to the counter and talked to one of the policemen.

Sharon's mother and my parents came in next.

Kenny flew into Mother's arms, yelling, "Mama, Mama, Mama!" She picked him up and they walked over to our bench.

Sharon and I interrupted each other trying to tell the story. We put in the part about Diane thumbing the ride. Diane's mother was sitting right on the bench with us, and when she heard that, she raised one eyebrow and looked at Diane.

Sharon's mother said quietly to my mother, "I hope they get Robyn in time."

I spoke up. "What will happen if they don't?"

Mother patted my head. "Don't worry. The police will find her."

The police station door flew open. Elsie's mother swished through and went straight to the counter. She and the policeman talked together for a long time. When the policeman left the counter to answer the phone, Elsie's mother walked over to our bench and said coldly to Elsie, "This is it for you, Elsie."

I felt a shudder move through Elsie. I put my arm around her. Her mother walked to the opposite wall. She stood there by herself with her arms folded and her head facing the counter. My mother put Kenny down and went over to Mrs. Edwards. She talked softly to her. Mrs. Edwards reached in her purse for her hanky and carefully wiped under each eye. I thought she was pretty. She had yellow curly hair and a dimple like Elsie. Only she wasn't fat like Elsie. She was very, very skinny.

"I'm starving," Sharon told her mother.

Sharon's mother leaned over to Diane's mother. "Do you suppose we should feed them?"

Diane's mother said, "Let's wait a little longer."

Kenny crawled up in Daddy's lap and fell asleep.

The policeman left the counter to talk with Mrs. Edwards. I wondered what he was saying. Mother returned to our bench, smiling. "They've got Robyn. She's O.K."

Elsie let out a big breath.

"Good," Sharon said. "Now we can eat."

We all stood up, stretched, and got ready to leave. Before we reached the door, Elsie's little sister bounced through, licking an orange Popsicle and swinging her red purse. She was followed by the truck driver and a state patrolman. The truck driver and the patrolman went on through the No Admittance door. Mrs. Edwards swooped up Robyn into her arms.

"Are you all right? Are you all right?" Mrs. Edwards asked.

"Sure," Robyn said. There were dried tearstains on her cheeks, but the Popsicle seemed to have erased them from her memory.

Mrs. Edwards peered into her daughter's face. "What did he do to you?"

Robyn held up the dripping stick. "The policeman bought me this."

"No," Mrs. Edwards said. "What did the truck driver do to you?"

"Nothing. I was just sitting in the back of the truck and a patrol car came up and hollered on his loudspeaker to pull over, so the truck driver did. Then the policeman brought us here in his car."

Cats Go Out at Night

After we left the police station, our family went out to dinner. Mother ordered Kenny a plain little hamburger. I ordered a big juicy one with all the fixings. I asked Daddy what the police would do to the truck driver.

"Maybe nothing," Daddy said, "if he has a good excuse for being out that far."

"Poor Elsie," I said, "her mother's so mad at her she's going to send her away to boarding school."

Mother looked at me sternly. "Elsie was supposed to be watching her little sister. I'm not too pleased about your going off with Kenny without permission."

I paid attention to my hamburger. I didn't want to get into that subject.

"I guess your job isn't worth all this trouble, eh?" my father said to my mother.

"Or your bowling isn't worth all this trouble," my mother said to my father.

Things were pretty quiet on the way home. When I got out of the car, I called D.D. I figured she would be hungry. I expected to see her come swishing around the house with her tail up. She didn't. I called and called. I looked in the backyard and out behind the garage. Finally Daddy yelled at me to get in the house and go to bed.

I lay in bed awake a long time. I was tired, but I wasn't sleepy. I wondered what was happening to Elsie. I wondered where my cat was. I really liked them both very much. Finally I did fall asleep, but then I was awakened by howling and screeching outside my window. I got up and peered into the outside darkness. I could see three animals race across the lawn. I couldn't tell if one was D.D. I hoped she wasn't hurt.

The next morning was Sunday. I lolled in my bed, watching the sun stream through my window. The smell of pancakes was drifting up from the kitchen. The ride in the truck seemed as if it had happened in a movie. I stretched and thought of butter and syrup oozing over pancakes. D.D.! D.D. hadn't come home! I hurried out of bed and into the bathroom. I went down the stairs to the kitchen, hoping she'd come when I called.

She did! She hopped up the back steps, walked through the door as if she'd never been gone, sat down on the kitchen floor, and proceeded to lick her messed-up fur.

I crouched beside her. "Where have you been, D.D.?"

Daddy, Mother, and Kenny were at the kitchen table, eating. "How old's that cat?" Daddy asked Mother.

"Oh, a little over six months," Mother said.

"Fine," Daddy said sarcastically. "Did you get her spayed?"

"No, did you?" Mother asked. She was certainly standing up to Daddy since she got her job. I thought that was neat.

I held D.D. in my arms. "Do you think she's going to be a mama?"

"Many times," Daddy replied.

Peace Talks

On Monday it seemed that school took forever. I was anxious to get out so I could find out from Elsie what happened after we left the police station. School wouldn't have been so boring if Mrs. Hanson had let us do crafts like we did in the fourth grade or let us make a movie like the sixth graders were doing. But she just liked us to be in our seats, working quietly. I wished she had retired before we got her.

After school half the class crowded around Elsie in the school yard. Jack wanted to know what the police did to the truck driver. I wanted to know first what was going to happen to Elsie. We were all pushing and talking to her at once.

"Shut up," Diane told everybody. "I want to know what happened."

Jack ignored her. "Tell us about the truck driver, Elsie."

"He told the police that he was going out to Snohomish to get a horn for his truck," Elsie said, "and that he was coming back to Lynnwood to the shopping center. He said he thought we kids would enjoy the ride."

Diane put her hands on her hips. "Well, then how come he didn't answer us when you pounded on the window?"

"He said he had his radio on. He said he didn't even know we'd jumped out of the truck until the State Patrol stopped him."

"Did the police buy all that?" Jack asked.

Elsie shrugged. "I don't know."

"My mother said he's just lucky he didn't drive over a state line or he'd have been in real trouble," Sharon said. Sharon always tells everybody what her mother says. If you know Sharon, you can get pretty sick of what her mother says.

"So nothing happened to him?" Jack persisted.

"The police gave him a ticket for driving without a horn."

"Cripes," Lester said, "he got off easy."

"You girls were sure dumb to get in that truck," Jack told us.

I didn't want to hear about that. I wanted to hear what Elsie's mother was going to do to her. "Is your mother going to send you away?"

Elsie looked down at the playground and kicked some of the gravel around. "I have to leave in June for a boarding school summer camp."

"That's only a month away," Marianne said.

The boys left. They didn't care what happened to Elsie. We girls started walking home. Marianne went partway with us. She reached out and took Elsie's hand and swung their hands between them as they walked. I felt like telling Marianne we were too old to hold hands.

Diane, Elsie, and I sat around Diane's kitchen table with our arithmetic books closed. There was only one more week of fractions. We didn't really need to have Elsie teach us any more, but my mother said we should finish the week out together. She was enjoying all my hundreds.

Diane plunked the ice up and down in her glass of grape juice with her fingers. "Couldn't you just explain to your mother that it wasn't your fault your sister got back in the truck?"

Elsie shook her head. "Mama doesn't listen to me explain. She explains to me—why I am going."

From what I saw of Mrs. Edwards, I believed that. "You need a grown-up to talk to her," I said. "How about your mother, Diane?"

"Not *my* mother," Diane replied. *"Your* mother. She's the one who can talk people into things."

It was true. My mother could sweet-talk anyone. Already, at work, she was selling more plants in a day than any other clerk in the nursery.

My mother was making dinner when I got home. I helped her cut the vegetables for salad to get her in a good mood. While I sliced a tomato, I asked casually, "Do you think you could visit Mrs. Edwards?"

"I suppose I could, but why should I?" she asked. She was putting the fish in the broiler.

I waited until she finished. "I don't think Elsie's mother understands that Elsie couldn't get her sister out of that truck."

"I think Mrs. Edwards understands she's got real problems with both Elsie and that little girl."

"Mother, she doesn't have a problem with Elsie any more. She just thinks she does. Elsie drinks grapefruit juice when we drink grape juice. She never touches any extra food. Mother, you can get anybody to listen to you. You could try Mrs. Edwards."

"O.K., I'll give it a try." She peeked in the oven to see how the fish was doing.

I was stunned that she had agreed so fast. I'd hardly

gotten into my argument. "When will you go?" I asked.

"Oh, tomorrow I might have time." She took the lid off the pan of steaming green beans. "I think we're about ready. Let's get this food on the table."

My mother wasn't there when I came home the next afternoon. I hoped she was with Mrs. Edwards. I set the table and put some potatoes in the oven to bake. She arrived as I was standing in the middle of the kitchen trying to decide what else I could do for her. I hurried out to the living room.

"Did you visit Mrs. Edwards?"

"Yes," she said. She was taking off Kenny's sweater and shooing him into the bathroom.

"Did it work?" I asked.

"Nope."

"Why not?" I sat down on Daddy's big chair. I couldn't believe it.

Mother sat down on the davenport. "Jenifer, Elsie was suspended from her last school and she is remaining in this school only on probation."

"I know that, Mother. But why does she have to be sent away?"

"Elsie has to go to school somewhere."

"Maybe Mr. Douglas will let her come back to our school in the fall."

"Maybe he will and maybe he won't."

"Why couldn't Mrs. Edwards at least try?"

Mother sighed. "I don't know why. I think she may have given up on Elsie."

"I think she has, too, and that isn't fair."

"Well, Jenifer, one of the things you're going to find out in life is that you can't straighten out other people's lives if they don't want you to. And I don't think Mrs. Edwards wants our advice. Maybe she would take somebody's. But I don't think she's going to take ours."

"Can I call Elsie on the phone and tell her it didn't work?" I asked. "She was hoping and hoping."

"You be careful what you say."

"I will," I promised.

I went to the phone and dialed Elsie's number. She answered.

"Hi, it's Jenny," I said. "I'm sorry, but my mother said it didn't work."

"I know," Elsie replied softly.

I waited a second. She didn't say any more, so I told her I'd see her tomorrow and hung up.

Walking home from school the next day, Diane was being discouraging. She didn't think anybody could convince Elsie's mother to keep her if my mother couldn't. I insisted my mother had said maybe Mrs. Edwards would take *somebody's* advice.

"My mother said," Sharon started in, "that your mother certainly seems to favor your little sister, Elsie."

"She does," Elsie said flatly.

We were walking by Chris Johnson's house. He and Mark Howard and some other sixth grade boys were tossing a basketball through a hoop in front of the garage. Chris Johnson held the ball as we passed. "Well, well, the terrible threesome has turned into three pins and a bowling ball."

"Naw," one of the other boys corrected him, "that's three asparagus spears and a yellow tomato."

I turned and screamed at them, "You shut up, Chris Johnson! You've got a humpy nose and pig eyes. You've got nothing to talk about."

Chris held the ball to his chest and, pretending he was overwhelmed, shrank backward into the other boys. "Why, Jenifer Sawyer, I didn't know you cared."

Diane laughed, but I didn't. They were so prejudiced. Just to show them, I held Elsie's hand as we walked away.

When the dinner dishes were finished, I went into the living room and sat down on the davenport with D.D. on my lap. Mother was crocheting beside me. "Do you think D.D.'s any fatter?" I asked.

Mother looked up from her crocheting. "She doesn't look any fatter to me."

"Don't worry. She will be," Daddy said from behind his paper.

"The sixth grade boys teased Elsie on the way home from school," I told mother. "They called her a yellow tomato and a bowling ball."

Daddy tipped his paper down, so he could see me. "Seems to me I remember your calling her 'that thief Elsie' a few months ago."

"I didn't know her then," I explained.

My father put his paper back up. "That's usually the way prejudice works."

I stroked D.D.'s sides. She seemed a little plumper to me.

The Old Lady Winked

The day of the school's spring concert, Elsie wore a new navy blue cotton pants suit. She said her mother made it for her. I thought that was a good sign. In P.E., Mr. Marshall noticed how nice she looked, too. We were standing with him while we waited for the boys' teams to finish their relay race.

"My, Elsie," he exclaimed, "you've lost a lot of weight. You're going to be absolutely skinny."

Elsie wasn't skinny yet, or even down to chubby, but she had lost that fat-lady-in-the-circus look.

"I won't be skinny until I lose a lot more pounds," Elsie told Mr. Marshall in her usual honest way.

"Ah, the rest will come off like skimming grease off chicken soup."

Elsie shook her head and looked down at her shoes. "It isn't that easy."

He patted her on the back. "You can do it, a smart girl like you." Mr. Marshall blew his whistle and our class lined up to return to our classroom and the spring concert.

Spring concerts are boring. All the orchestra kids get on the stage and squeak their violins and violas. When they're finished, they troop off and the band kids come on to struggle through Sousa marches. It takes an hour and a half. Before it's over, the little kids begin to wiggle and the bad older kids shove the chairs in front of them with their feet. There's a lot of "Cut it out!" until the teachers come down the aisles with mad faces to shush us up. As we file out of the gym, the teachers change their faces to smiles and nod at the performers' mothers, who sit in the back row.

Watching Mrs. Hanson greet Lester's mother gave me the idea. I dropped back to where Elsie was in line. "I've got an idea," I whispered to her. "Let's ask Mrs. Hanson to talk to your mother."

Elsie shook her head as we rounded the outside corner of the gym. "She won't listen."

"She'll have to," I insisted, "if Mrs. Hanson calls her in for a conference."

"Jenifer!" Mrs. Hanson called out sharply. "Since

you can't be quiet, come and walk with me."

I walked beside Mrs. Hanson silently until we almost got to the door of the fifth grade unit. Then I asked her if I could talk to her after school.

When our class had been dismissed, I brought my chair up beside Mrs. Hanson's desk. I'll say one thing about Mrs. Hanson—she's a good listener. I told her the whole story about the ride in the truck, Elsie's sister, and Elsie's diet. "Elsie has really tried," I explained. "It isn't fair."

I was fiddling with the calendar holder on Mrs. Hanson's desk as I talked. She reached over and put her hand on mine. "Jenifer, please don't say it isn't fair again. If there's one thing that makes me look forward to retirement, it's knowing I won't have to hear 'It isn't fair' any more."

"Oh. O.K." I put my hand in my lap. "It's just that Elsie has tried so hard and she's going to be sent away. She helped Diane and me with our math after school for a month."

"So that's it." Mrs. Hanson sat back in her chair, nodding. "That's the answer to your good papers. I was wondering."

"She's a very good teacher," I said.

"I imagine she is," Mrs. Hanson agreed.

"So couldn't you help her? You know how to say all those words to parents."

She looked at her calendar. "Well, maybe it is time for another conference with Mrs. Edwards. Let's see, today's Friday. You'll have gym again with Mr. Marshall next Tuesday. I'll talk with Mr. Douglas and see if we can set up a conference next Tuesday during gym time."

I got up to go. I thanked Mrs. Hanson twice for being so kind.

Tuesday was a long school day. We didn't have P.E. till the afternoon, so the whole morning had to be gotten through before Elsie's mother would even arrive at school. After lunch there was English before P.E. I had my usual trouble getting my paper started. Elsie wrote her paper quickly and spent the rest of the hour staring at a page in her library book and pulling on her hair. Toward the end of the hour I gave up and signed out for the bathroom. On the way back to the room, I peeked out the unit door. Mrs. Edwards' car was in the parking lot.

"She's here," I whispered to Elsie as I slid back in my seat.

Elsie nodded. There was no color in her face.

"Line up for P.E.," Mrs. Hanson ordered. "Quietly! Please."

Mr. Marshall had some sixth graders in the gym demonstrate tumbling to us. I thought Chris Johnson was the best tumbler. Diane thought Mark Howard was. I don't think Elsie cared.

Mrs. Edwards' car was gone from the parking lot when we left the gym to go back to the room. I grabbed Elsie's shoulder. "It's all decided now," I said.

Mrs. Hanson was at her desk when we entered the room. I looked carefully at her face as we marched to our seats to see if I could tell from her expression what the decision was. She winked at me. That old lady actually winked at me. I shoved Elsie in the back. She turned around, nodding. She had seen it, too.

During our reading lesson, Diane scribbled on a scrap of paper and passed it to me. The note said, "Did Mrs. Hanson wink at you???" I wrote on the bottom of the paper, "Yes," and handed it back. I leaned over and poked Elsie. When she looked up, I winked. She winked back. I felt so good I could have flown out the classroom window.

Elsie had to go to the doctor's after school so we didn't get the details of the conference until we met Elsie at school the next morning. We were barely at the school door when Diane and I climbed all over Elsie to tell us what Mrs. Hanson and her mother said.

"My mother said Mrs. Hanson said that I improved in behavior more than any other student she'd ever had."

"Do you get to stay? Do you get to stay?" I interrupted her.

"If the principal will let me back in the fall, I do."

"Will he?" I asked.

"He said I could try taking regular recesses with the kids, and if I didn't get in any more trouble, he would admit me in the fall. Mrs. Hanson said there were only two weeks left and she was sure I'd make it."

"Mrs. Hanson must have really laid it on," Diane said.

Elsie agreed. "She even told my mother that I was the top student in the class, and that I generously helped other students with their work."

"So that did it?" I asked.

"Well, Mama didn't say much on the way to the doctor. But when I got on the doctor's scale, we found I'd lost another four pounds, which made a total of thirty pounds."

"Thirty pounds!" I exclaimed. "I only weigh ninety."

Elsie looked at me wistfully. "I'd like to weigh ninety."

"You will," I told her. "We'll help you keep on your diet all next year."

"But you know my mother," Elsie warned. "If I do one little thing."

"Don't do anything, Elsie. Don't do *anything*," I told her.

"Don't worry," Elsie said. "I won't."

And she almost didn't.

I Can See My Shoes

The first week that Elsie had recess everything went smoothly. Then Diane got the brainstorm that she should teach Elsie to bat so we all could be on a softball team during the summer. Elsie was coordinated enough, but she didn't know anything about baseball. We took her way out to the edge of the playfield. I pitched the ball and Diane coached Elsie's swings.

Our action caught Jack's eye. He and some other boys in our room trooped over to watch. Every time Elsie swung and missed, Jack hollered, "Way to go!" Sweat came out on Elsie's forehead. I pitched. The boys counted, "One. Two. Three. Miss!"

Elsie bore down harder, trying to ignore them. The next pitch was outside. Elsie stumbled trying to get it. The ball just missed her head. Jack yelled behind her, "You're supposed to hit it, Fatty, not swallow it."

Elsie had had it. She whirled around, the bat still in her hand, and yelled, "Knock it off, Jack!"

I don't think Jack heard her. The bat had hit Jack in the mouth. He pitched forward onto the ground, his face landing in the gravel. Lester pulled him to a sitting position. Blood poured from Jack's lower lip. Elsie stared in horror, her face chalk white. This was it for Elsie. She hadn't meant to hit Jack, but that wasn't going to do her much good. If you fought on school grounds, the principal called your mother.

I saw the playground teacher hurrying toward us. I crouched down next to Jack. "Listen, Jack, if you say it was Elsie's fault, her mother will send her away to boarding school for good."

"Who cares where she goes." He was trying to wipe the blood from his mouth with the back of his hand. He only succeeded in smearing it across his face.

"Jack, please," I begged. "The principal might even kick Elsie out now because she's been in trouble before. Please, Jack."

The playground teacher pushed me away and kneeled down next to Jack. She took his chin in her hand and blotted the blood with a Kleenex. Jack's face was split from his lip to his chin.

"Come on. Let's get you to the nurse's office."

Sharon stepped forward. "Remember, Red, be a sport."

Jack glared at her and then wobbled away, holding his hand under his chin to catch the blood.

"What did you say that for?" I screamed at Sharon. "You know he hates being called Red."

"I was just trying to get him not to tell on Elsie."

"Get him not to tell! You made him mad!"

"Well, Jenny, you weren't getting anywhere. Don't scream at me." Sharon marched off in her prissy way.

I couldn't believe it. It was the dumbest thing to say. When Sharon tries to act big like Diane she always makes a mess of it.

I took Elsie by the arm. "Come on. Let's go sit on the bank above the backstop until recess is over."

We sat up there, or I sat up there. Elsie lay on her back with her arm across her eyes.

"Elsie," I asked, "why can't you stay with your dad instead of going to boarding school?"

Elsie took her arm away and stared up at the sky. "I dream about that all the time. But they're only dreams. That woman would never let him take me."

"You're not so fat any more. Maybe she would."

"And maybe she wouldn't." Elsie put her arm back over her eyes.

"You don't pig down any more. And you don't steal any more. Why wouldn't that woman want you now? Huh, Elsie?"

But she wouldn't answer me. She never believes anyone will like her.

During reading the intercom came on, and I thought for sure it was the office sending for Elsie. But instead the secretary asked Mrs. Hanson to send Jack's lunch box and books to the office. Lester carried them down.

After school we girls grabbed Lester.

"Where'd Jack go?"

"What happened to Jack?"

"Why didn't he come back to class?"

"Are you all nuts?" Lester said. "His mom took him to Stevens Hospital. The nurse said he'd have to have stitches."

When Elsie heard that, she walked off toward her house. I ran after her. "Wait a minute, Elsie. Maybe Jack won't tell."

Elsie plodded straight on.

I dragged on her arm. "Wait, Elsie. We'll go to Diane's and call Jack when he gets home."

She kept going.

"I don't think Jack will tell," Marianne said when I returned to the others. "Jack never tells on anyone."

"If Sharon hadn't called him Red," I said. "That was a dumb thing to say."

"Well, nobody's perfect," Sharon snapped.

At Diane's house we tried to call Jack eleven times, but there was no answer. Diane said you have to wait around forever at Stevens Hospital before a doctor sees you. I guess. I finally had to give up and go home.

I tried to talk to Mother about Elsie and Jack while we were alone in the kitchen, but she was rushing around making a cake for PTA and mumbling about the potatoes getting done so she could put the cake in the oven.

Dinner took forever. I caught Daddy watching me squish my peas on my plate. I hurried and stuffed a couple of big bites in my mouth and swallowed them whole. It was worth it not to ruin my chances of calling Jack and finding out if Elsie was doomed. Daddy was the one with the rule about no phone calls.

I waited until he was watching a baseball game on TV before I started explaining about the accident to Mother. Daddy heard the part about my wanting to call Jack, though, and interrupted me. "You see your friends all day. You don't need to talk to them at night."

Mother gave Daddy her sweetest smile. "Well, maybe, in this special case we might let her use the phone for five minutes. What do you think?"

He looked confused for a minute.

The TV announcer was saying, "There it goes! It's over the left field fence!"

"All right," Daddy said quickly. "Five minutes and no more." And he got back to his ball game.

I dived for the phone. Boy, was I glad Mother started making her own decisions. Jack's mother answered. She didn't sound too pleased. Neither was Jack when he found out it was me.

"How's your lip?" I asked him.

"I got six stitches on account of your dumb friend, and it hurts to talk."

"Did you tell on Elsie?"

"What do you think I am, a narc? Listen, I have to go."

"O.K.," I said. "Thanks a lot for saving Elsie. Now she'll get to stay in our school next year."

"Big deal," he said and hung up.

I hurried and dialed Elsie's number. Her mother must have been out because she answered.

"Elsie," I said, "I talked to Jack and he didn't tell." She didn't say anything.

"Elsie, are you still there?"

"Yes. It's just that I've been so scared." Her voice sounded funny. I wondered if she was pulling on her hair like she always does when she's nervous.

"Maybe we better stay in the library during recess until school's over on Friday," I told her. "Then nothing else bad can happen to you."

Elsie agreed, so that's what we did. She and I

trooped off to the library every recess until Friday. We didn't mind because we both liked to read. My favorite book was *The Best Christmas Pageant Ever*. Elsie had read all the animal stories in the library, and her favorite was *Savage Sam*. I promised her a kitten when D.D. had her babies.

Mrs. Hanson gave us our report cards just before school was dismissed. We had our class party, cleaned the room, and fifth grade was about over. Mrs. Hanson's hair was mussed and her skin sagged around her mouth, but she smiled at each of us and said good-bye, have a nice summer, as she handed us our report cards. When she came to Elsie, she told her there was a note from the principal with her report card and she was glad Elsie was coming back next year.

I yelled, "Yippee!" and hugged Elsie and Elsie hugged me before we even got out the classroom door.

"Elsie, read the note," Diane ordered when we were clear of the school building.

We crowded around Elsie and read the principal's note together. Mr. Douglas had written that, because of Elsie's exemplary behavior the past few months, he would be pleased to have her return to the school next fall.

"What does 'exemplary' mean?" Sharon asked.

"Who cares?" I said. "She gets to stay." I was busy pulling out my own report card. I got a B in arithmetic. So did Diane. Elsie got an A.

Diane skipped ahead. "Let's go swimming," she said.

Elsie was walking along looking at her shoes. I had noticed her looking at her shoes a lot the past month. I asked her why she was always staring at her feet.

"I can see my shoes," she said, smiling.

"Everybody can see their shoes," I said.

"No, they can't. I couldn't for two years."

"Were you really that fat?" Sharon asked.

"I was fat," Elsie answered. "Let's face it. I wasn't just fat. I was gross."

"And we were mean," I said. I was ashamed to remember how I had treated Elsie.

"You were," Elsie agreed. "But I was all mouth."

"Come on, you pokes!" Diane called ahead of us. "It's hot. Let's get in the water."

I took Elsie's hand. We ran to catch up.